Someone tried to kill me.

The reality of the situation hit Kelly and she collapsed onto her bed, shaking. I could have died! she thought. Really *died*! Someone tried to kill me.

After a long time the shakes lessened and she tried to think. Did someone really try to kill me? Could it have been an accident? I don't think so.

I can't think why someone would want to hurt me. But someone does. Someone hates me. Someone who is getting more serious.

But *who* is it?

point

FINAL EXAM

A. Bates

SCHOLASTIC INC.
New York Toronto London Auckland Sydney

ISBN 0-590-43291-5

12 11 10 9   3 4 5/9

Printed in the U.S.A.   01

First Scholastic printing, May 1990

This book is dedicated with love and thanks
to Grover and Shirin
without whom nothing would have been possible.

With special thanks to Clint
for the mechanical puzzle.

Monday

1

Here I sit looking down on the world.

No one can see me up here.

What if I get caught?

I won't get caught. I can't turn back now. Not without getting the test. A winner never quits and a quitter never wins. Remember?

But I can pass English without that test. It's wrong to steal. And I didn't know it would be such a long way down. Why am I doing this?

I can't just pass, I have to win. Besides, it's not that far down. All I have to do is hold on and step down onto the filing cabinet. Just like I planned. I can do it. I have to do it.

Wait a minute. I thought that door would be closed. In my plan it was closed. What if someone comes by? What if someone sees me?

A winner does what must be done.

And this must be done.

2

"At least I'll make the history books," Kelly said, tipping her hat brim up to give Talia a bleak look. "The first person to die from finalitis. People will have to study *me*. That's poetic justice."

"Kelly!" Talia said. "Nobody ever died from taking finals. It just doesn't happen."

"I said I'd be the first," Kelly said. They headed up the hall, surrounded by the familiar between-class flow of people and noise.

Talia's green eyes lightened as she waved to friends, then sobered as they returned to Kelly. "Finals are guaranteed to be nonfatal," she said. "People may flunk, but they survive. It can't have been that bad."

"Remember that stop sign I waited at this morning?" Kelly asked. "When you said go, and I said I didn't want to go because then I'd wind up here and have to take my History final?"

"Yeah."

"I should have turned."

"History's tough," Talia said. "The other tests will be easier."

"It wasn't that it was hard," Kelly said, stopping at her locker. She spun the dial quickly. "I froze." She lowered her voice. "I panicked. I couldn't read. I couldn't even pick up my pencil."

She shoved books and folders onto the locker shelf and grabbed her Spanish text. "All I could think of was my English final last year." She slammed the locker door, and she and Talia continued up the hall.

"I only want one thing," Kelly continued. "I want to make it through this week alive. And sane. And I want to pass my finals. All of them."

"That's three things, at least," Talia pointed out.

"See? I can't even count anymore," Kelly said. "I tell you, by Friday I'll be nothing but a walking rhododendron, slobbering and biting itself."

Talia laughed. "I think you mean a mad dog," she said. "A rhododendron's a flower. Or a bush. It's a plant, anyway. Plants don't slobber."

"I told you," Kelly said. "I'm degenerating rapidly. Mad dogs and flowers . . . it's all the same. I can't tell the difference. Oops, I almost forgot. I'd better see if the office has those forms. Meet you in class."

Kelly watched as Talia's blonde hair and slim form disappeared into the crowd of students on the stairs. Then she turned aside, down a wide hall that ended at a glass-paneled door. Seven final exams, she thought. This is going to be a tough week for seniors. Our whole future's on the line. Whether we pass, graduate, get into college — it all depends on how we do this one week.

Kelly pushed the office door open and stopped at the counter. "Did the job directory forms come in?" she asked.

The student aide looked up from the pages of the newsletter he was assembling. "Don't tell me," he said. "I'm testing a new memory trick. Let's see." He leaned his elbows on the counter, staring at her. "Derby hat. Black hair. Blue eyes. You must be my date for Tad's party."

"What is this, love at first sight?" Kelly asked. "I thought it was a senior's party. Are you invited?"

"I will be if you invite me," he said.

Kelly grinned. "I see," she said. "An opportunist. Sorry. No date. Did you get the job directory forms yet?"

"If you won't go out with me, I'm not going to tell you. Besides, I don't remember. You can go look. I've got a ton of work to do before I can eat lunch."

"It's only refried hamburgers anyway," Kelly said, skirting the counter on the far side. "No big loss." At the rear of the office she turned right, into a short hall ending in an alcove. On her left was a storage room of some kind, to her right the copy and paper room, and ahead, in the alcove, a table loaded with forms.

The final bell for fourth period rang as Kelly scanned the papers on the table. She located the student job directory forms, grabbed one and turned, heading back.

Something in the storage room caught her attention but when Kelly looked, she couldn't tell what she had noticed.

I thought something moved, she thought, frowning. Or did I hear something?

Ignoring the No Students sign on the open door she detoured into the room for a closer look. The only thing out of place amid the crowded shelves, filing cabinets, and boxes was a small brown book on the floor, a book the size of a miniature address book.

Kelly picked it up. *Winners* was embossed in gold letters on the front. Curious, she opened it, flipping pages. There was one inspirational message printed on each page in large, gold letters. "I am a winner. Winners win," was the message on the first page. Not too original, Kelly thought. She thumbed to another page. "Losers are going nowhere. Where are you going?" it said. Beneath the printing was a blank space that had been filled in with hand-scrawled notes and scribbled personal comments about some of the teachers.

I don't think I'd better turn this in to Lost and Found, Kelly decided. Not with the comments about the teachers in it! I wouldn't want anyone to see this if it were mine. Maybe I can figure out whose it is and give it back. I don't recognize the hand-writing. It's just scribbles. Nothing distinctive.

She dropped the book in her book bag, stopping by the counter again on the way out. "I'll need a pass," she said. "To get back into class."

"Forget it," the aide told her.

3

"What?" Kelly asked.

"Opportunists don't write passes," the aide said. "Besides, every senior in school is stopping by for something today. I've got more to do than write a thousand admits."

Kelly tipped her hat forward and leaned her elbows on the counter. "So I should take detention for being late?"

"You could," he said, grinning. "Or you could tell the teacher to buzz the office if he asks for a pass. But I bet he won't. You seniors got it made this week. Nobody expects you to do a darned thing except take a few tests."

"Right," Kelly told him. Take a few tests! she thought. What am I doing this week? Oh, nothing much. Just taking a few final exams. Just deciding my whole future, that's all. I'd rather take an entire car apart with a screwdriver and put it back together again. Ten cars! Of course, I'd rather do that than just about anything else, anyway.

* * *

After school Kelly hurried to the parking lot to drop off her books before meeting Talia. Talia wanted to watch the baseball team, and since Kelly was giving her a ride home, she'd reluctantly agreed to stay.

I hope it's just a practice and not a real game, Kelly thought. Then maybe I can talk Talia into leaving early. I need to get home and study. Did I get all my books?

She rummaged through her pack, checking.

Oh, she thought, coming across the little brown book. *Winners.* I should ask around about it. Someone might know whose it is.

She slipped it in the pocket of her windbreaker. Geometry and Computer Literacy finals tomorrow, she thought, looking at her textbooks. I've got all I need, I guess.

She ran her hand briefly over the polished finish of the hood of her 1960 Thunderbird. She'd bought the rusted-out heap for $150, then had put uncounted hours into rebuilding and refinishing it, working painstakingly until the sleek machine reemerged from the ruins.

Beautiful, she thought, rubbing a smudge off the fender. You are beautiful.

She tossed her book bag in the car and ran back to the school.

"Go on and save seats," Talia told her. "I'll get us some food. Nachos okay?"

"Sure." Kelly headed out to the bleachers. After a few minutes, members of the baseball team began straggling onto the field in twos and threes, joking and tossing the ball back and forth. The stands began to fill up with classmates and parents.

Where's Talia? Kelly thought. It doesn't take that long to buy nachos.

The players gathered together, stretching and warming up. Finally Kelly saw Talia making her way toward the bleachers with a cardboard tray in each hand.

"Thanks," Kelly said, taking the nachos and Coke Talia handed her. "What took you so long?"

"I ran into Jeffrey," Talia said, choosing a cheesy chip. "Are you going to Tad's party?"

Kelly shrugged. "Haven't decided," she said. "It sounds like fun. Swimming, barbecue, and dancing. And right after finals is a perfect time. We'll need something like that to let off steam after this week! But . . . I'm not sure I'll want to see some of the people who might be there."

"Might be?" Talia asked. "Trust me, Kelly. If there's a particular somebody you don't want to see, Danny will be there. Guaranteed."

"I didn't mention any names!" Kelly said. She scooped some cheese out of the corner where it had pooled.

"It was implied," Talia said, scanning the field. "I understood, anyway."

The bleachers were nearly full. Even though it turned out to be only a practice game, the team drew a regular crowd. They'd had a winning season, taking the league title and winning the district playoffs, extending the season to include the state tournament in a few weeks.

The players had taken positions around the field, getting serious about their practice, the slap of balls into mitts sounding firm and definite.

"There's Tad now," Talia said, pointing. "I wonder why he's so late."

"Everybody's late to everything these days," Kelly said. "I thought I was late to Spanish, but half the class trickled in after I got there. Including you. And you should have been ahead of me because I stopped off to get forms."

"I got to class on time," Talia said, finishing her nachos. "But nobody was there, so I wandered around. Far be it from me to sit alone in an empty classroom. Well, I was looking for Jeff, actually. I mean, what's the point in going together if I never see him?"

"You'd have seen him in class," Kelly pointed out.

"That's not exactly what I had in mind," Talia said.

"Are you and Jeff going to the party?" Kelly asked, watching the players gather equipment after their warm-up, tossing balls into their dugout.

"I guess I'm going if Jeff goes. And whether he goes depends on his finals. If he doesn't ace them, I don't know if he'll feel like partying. I swear, everybody's whole life depends on this week. Except Tad's, maybe. He's got everything aced already. How can anyone have such a perfect life? Tad Sedalia — star athlete, rich, popular, good-looking, *and* a science whiz. It isn't fair."

"He's not so hot," Kelly said. "I mean, does he

have a derby hat and can he fix cars? A person like that is really big time."

"You may not believe this, Kelly, but a whole lot of people are impressed by things like being rich and smart and good-looking. They actually think that's more important than a hat, or a tune-up, or a brake job."

"I hadn't realized," Kelly said, adjusting her hat brim to shade her eyes as she watched the field. "So that's why business has been slow."

"Of course, *your* hat is important," Talia said. "It's a statement."

"It's not a statement," Kelly said. "It's my hat."

"Well, it's not a fashion statement, that's for sure," Talia said, grinning. "Nobody but you wears a hat like that. But, Kelly, when someone wears something that has no purpose, it's a statement of some kind."

"Actually, calling it a statement is one of the kinder things you could have said," Kelly told her. "My sister says it's my security blanket. My mother says it's ugly. I just say it's my hat."

"I won't argue with that. But don't worry about business being slow. It's because of finals. People are putting everything else off. After this week you'll have more business than you can handle."

"Good. I'm planning to pay tuition with what I earn. Becoming a mechanic isn't cheap."

"Becoming one? What are you now?"

"I'm practicing to be a mechanic. I've got a lot to learn. I can't believe how much is computer-regulated these days! Those little chips change everything! Did you ever stop and think — ?"

"Um . . . Kelly?" Talia interrupted.

"Oops. Sorry." Kelly grinned at her friend. "Scared you, huh? Okay, I'll think of something non-mechanical to talk about. What was Jeff up to, anyway? I don't see him out here cheering our team to greater glory."

"Actually, he's going to the library to study. He said I shouldn't tell anyone because he doesn't want to blow his image. But you won't tell him I told, right?"

"I swear. I will not say a word. But it is an intriguing thought. I didn't know Jeffrey got serious long enough to do things like studying. Actually, I guess Jeff doesn't have to get serious," Kelly said. "He may clown around, but he always knows the answers."

The first batter took his position, the second was warming up on deck.

"Jeff's doing pretty well in all his classes," Talia agreed. "But the pressure's on him, too. Just like everyone else. Acceptance to college is always conditional. You have to make the grade right up to graduation. Especially for a place like Dartmouth. Everyone's praying this week. Except maybe Tad. He's been accepted to MIT, of course. Did we expect less?"

"Now get out there and kill 'em!" shouted a man below them in the bleachers. "Play like you're serious!"

Talia made a face. "Speaking of Tad," she whispered. "That may be the only blight on his life. His father is kind of obnoxious. I wonder what he'd have done if Tad hadn't been accepted to MIT."

"I think it's nice he cares," Kelly said. "That's one of the worst things about having divorced parents. Seems like one of them winds up moving away. And since Dad's a traveling mechanic he never stays anywhere long enough to visit. If I were playing baseball I'd want my father at the games."

"Just listen," Talia told her.

Kelly watched Tad's father as he leaned forward to shout at the fielders. "Get the lead out! What d'you think? The ball's going to float into your glove? You've got to run for it! *Now* you move! Last week would have been better!"

"You'd think he was the coach instead of just a parent," Talia said. "And this is only practice. I've heard him at some of the games. I can't believe how involved he gets. Just our luck to sit so close to him."

Kelly listened to the crowd shouting around her. "They're all pretty involved," she said. "This is the first time we've had a team make it to state. Everyone takes it personally."

"You're playing baseball!" Tad's father shouted. "Not Simon Says."

Kelly winced.

Later she said, "You're right, Tee. It's the fourth inning and he hasn't slowed down. If I were Tad I think I'd tell him to stay home."

"It's not always easy telling fathers anything," Talia said, sounding gloomy. "I hardly get any time with Jeff anymore. My dad's always after me to study, study, study. Well, to be fair, his folks are just as bad. They're pretty proud he's going to Dartmouth."

"Studying is not bad advice," Kelly said. "I could use a little book time, myself. Do you need to stick around for the rest of this or could we possibly leave early?"

They stood and edged their way to the aisle and climbed down the bleachers, heading for the student parking lot in back of the school.

"I can't believe Jeff," Talia said. "I guess he got in trouble today. He filled some teacher's desk drawers with popcorn — unbuttered, thankfully — and then got hungry after gym, so he stopped off to eat some. It never occurred to him that that would be an admission of guilt, knowing it was in there." They tossed their trash into a can as they passed.

"It's a good thing Jeff's a good student," Talia added. "If you're a good student you get away with a lot more. I can't believe some of the things he does."

A light wind kicked up, briefly, and Kelly held onto her hat with one hand, watching the windblown debris scuttle along the edge of the school and then lie still again. "Once Jeff gets to Dartmouth, he'll probably slow down a little," she said. "It's a good school. He'll have to get serious if he's going to do as well there as he does here."

"I know. I hate the thought of college, Kel." Talia sounded tired. "Sometimes I think it's something parents dreamed up. Nobody in their right mind would want to do this for four more years."

"If you don't want to go, then why are you?" Kelly asked.

Talia looked exasperated. "You don't understand at all, do you? You don't even realize how lucky you are. You've not only got a natural talent, it's one your parents approve of. You just go ahead and do what you want without worrying about what anyone else thinks. Not everyone has that luxury."

"Dad approves of my skills, anyway," Kelly said. "And Mom has Susan."

"When your parents are the ones paying for college, it isn't easy to go against what they want," Talia went on. "Be glad you're paying for yourself. No one can tell you what to do. You're your own boss. Oh, and speaking of your job, I wish Jeff would bring his car over for you to look at."

"What's wrong with it?" Kelly and Talia rounded the corner of the school, heading across the tennis courts toward the gate to the parking lot.

"Oh, it kind of lurches along sometimes. Chugging and whining. Almost like it's turning itself off and back on real fast, and complaining the whole time."

"Is it an electronic ignition?" Kelly asked.

Talia looked thoughtful. "Gee, Kelly," she said, mock-serious. "I didn't think to ask. Especially since I never heard the words used together before. I mean, I've heard electronic. And I've heard ignition. That's where you put the key. Jeff's car takes a key to operate, so I'd say it's a key-driven ignition, not electronic."

"Tell Jeff to bring it over anytime," Kelly said, laughing.

"It'll probably be a while," Talia said, smiling back. "He's pretty busy right now."

"Yeah," Kelly agreed. "But you'll both wish you'd had it looked at if you get stuck in the middle of nowhere."

"Why is your car door open?" Talia asked, pointing. "What's that all over it?"

No, Kelly thought, racing for the T-bird. Not my car! She stopped short, staring in dismay at the white-and-yellow goo splattering her car inside and out.

4

"Eggs!" Talia said. "How sick! This is disgusting!"

"It's worse than that," Kelly muttered, looking in horror at the mess on her glove compartment maps and receipts, and on her books and papers, which were strewn everywhere, lying in an eggy mess. "I'd like to say a few choice words right about now. And I'd like to wring someone's neck."

Danny? she thought, reaching in the pocket of her jeans for the keys. Could Danny have done this? She remembered the last time she'd talked to him . . . his clenched fists. "I said I was sorry, Kelly," he'd said. "What more do you want? Blood?"

"I'll say them for you," Talia offered. "The choice words, I mean."

"Go right ahead. Please." Kelly unlocked the trunk.

"What are you going to do?" Talia asked.

"Clean it," Kelly said. "What else can I do?" She started unloading the trunk, her anger mounting as the eggs hardened and dried in the sun. She put her toolboxes on the ground, a droplight, a box of spare parts, setting aside a gallon of water, rags, and a small shovel.

She and Talia set to work, scooping eggs off the seat and floor with the shovel, dumping water from the jug onto rags and wiping the mess as best they could.

"This makes me sick," Kelly said, her voice tight, angry. "Why would anyone do this? It's like they did it to *me*, you know? Threw eggs in *my* face. This car is my baby. Everybody knows that. Who could hate me that much?"

"I hear Danny's pretty mad, Kelly," Talia said, wiping egg off the roof of the car. "Don't overlook the obvious. He's not the most even-tempered guy I've ever seen."

"I don't think it was Danny," Kelly said slowly, dabbing her Geometry book. "Or maybe I just hope it wasn't."

"You sound like you're defending him," Talia said.

"He has good qualities, too, you know," Kelly said. "His temper isn't one of them, but there's more to him than that."

Talia paused in her work. "Do I hear doubts?" she asked.

Kelly shook her head. "I did the right thing breaking up with him. But I don't think he did this. He's pretty direct, Talia. He might have kicked out a headlight or something, but I don't know about eggs."

She wiped at her notes, wondering if she'd be

able to read them. "Of course, he's not dumb, either," she added thoughtfully. "I mean, he had to know if I found my window punched out again, I'd know who did it."

Talia's eyes widened. "He did *what?*"

"Oops," Kelly said. "I wasn't going to say anything. Forget it, will you?"

"He punched out the T-bird's window?" Talia said, her voice rising in disbelief. "Kelly! I thought you broke up with him because you got smart. I thought you finally got tired of his temper. Honestly! I can't believe it took an assault on your car to make you wise up!"

"Can we forget it?" Kelly asked. "He's been under a lot of pressure. If he doesn't bring his English grade up he might not make it into the Academy. He only got conditional acceptance. He's edgy and we were arguing and he punched the window. It could have happened to anyone."

"You know what," Talia asked, tossing her rag to Kelly. "It still sounds to me like you've got some doubts. You sound like you're making excuses for Danny. 'It could have happened to anyone'? Really, Kel."

"I don't have any doubts. Well, maybe a couple," Kelly said, rinsing the rags in water from her gallon jug. She looked up. "No, no doubts at all. I'm sure. It's over. And I don't think he did the eggs." I hope, she added silently, sighing.

Talia gathered and organized papers while Kelly repacked the trunk. They both eyed the leather bucket seats before they climbed in, checking suspiciously for bits of shell or slimy egg white they might have missed.

Kelly fired the engine, thrilling as always to the smooth, instant power.

Talia fiddled with the levers on the console between the seats, then switched the radio on. "I'm glad you upgraded the sound system," she said. "This is a great old car but they sure didn't know how to make radios in those days. Or tape players. Or CD players, either. You should put a CD player in here. Kelly, you're lucky nobody stole your sound system. Why didn't you lock the car?"

"I didn't think I had to lock it at school," Kelly said. "Who locks anything at school?" She frowned. "Why didn't they steal the tape player?"

"Don't ask me," Talia said.

"I think that's pretty strange. Why would someone vandalize the car and not steal the stereo?"

"You were lucky," Talia said. "Maybe someone came and scared them off. Maybe they didn't know how to take the stereo out. I wouldn't know how to steal one. You'd better be more careful about locking up."

Kelly sighed. "I suppose I'll have to," she agreed.

Kelly slowed for a turn, then sped up again. "Next week I'll change my habits," she said. "This week I'm just trying to survive. Maybe someone will open a people tune-up shop, Tee. I could go in and have my memory adjusted. Or my tension meter. Maybe I should just have a complete overhaul done on my entire nervous system. It's been going haywire lately."

"Ease up on yourself," Talia said. "So you flunked one English final. Last year. You were sick. You missed a lot of school. But you didn't flunk any other finals, last year or any other year. So relax and quit going crazy. Do you want me to help you study tonight?"

Kelly made the turn into Talia's subdivision. "No thanks," she said, shaking her head. "I've got Computer Literacy and Geometry. You can't help with Computer Lit. The only thing that would help is if I had a computer at home. Or at least the keyboard. Geometry is just drill and theorems. I'll manage."

"You'll do fine, Kelly," Talia said, getting out of the Thunderbird. "I know you will. Keep it in perspective. It's just tests. Just a few final exams. Thanks for the ride."

"Sure," Kelly said. She drove home through the late-spring afternoon, the air faintly perfumed with flowering shrubs and the scent of new-mown lawns.

Give me a nice, clean, mechanical problem any day, she thought. I'm not very good at anything else. Danny, for instance. Finals, for instance. I think I'll swear off guys. And I'm definitely going to swear off finals. At least after this week. So all I have to do is make it through this week.

She sighed, thinking of the six finals that still awaited her. Then she grinned. Talia said nobody ever died from taking finals, she reminded herself. I won't either.

5

"If it isn't Daddy's little girl," Susan said as Kelly walked in the front door.

Kelly adjusted her hat brim, then wished she hadn't. Conditioned response, she thought. She says Dad, I touch the hat.

Susan's expression was smug.

Kelly looked at Susan. She could never decide whether her sister was beautiful or merely pretty. Almost seventeen, only one year behind her in school, Susan was tall and willowy-slim like their mother, with the same black hair worn in long, loose waves. She and Kelly had the same parents, the same dark hair, both had wound up in the same Spanish class.

And that's where the similarity ends, Kelly thought. That's all we have in common.

"Have you seen Grease?" she asked.

Susan nodded. "Yes, I fed her for you. She's almost out of cat food," she said. "Dad called," she added, looking like it hurt her to admit it.

Oh, Kelly thought, mentally changing gears. That's why she's being touchy.

"He was very disappointed that you weren't home," Susan said.

"Oh," Kelly said. "Well, I'm sorry I missed him. But I'm sure he enjoyed talking to you."

"Oh, yeah, we had a great conversation," Susan told her. " 'Where's Kelly? Gee, I thought she'd be home by now. Well, Suzie, darling, would you take a message for your sister? Would you ask her how she'd like to work the races with me this summer? I was bragging about her mechanical skills and darned if old George didn't offer her a job. Can you beat that? Ask her for me, won't you, Suze? Don't forget. I can't think of a better way to spend the summer than having one of my girls working beside me.' "

Susan glared at Kelly, daring her to say something.

Kelly couldn't think of a thing to say. She knew Susan was hurt. But she wouldn't want to get her hands greasy, Kelly thought. Even if she knew where to find a spark plug and how to change it — which she doesn't — she couldn't go work with Dad. The idea's ridiculous!

"Are you going to?" Susan asked.

Kelly shrugged. "I don't know. It'll probably depend on the money they're willing to pay. I have to earn my tuition. And buy tools. I make pretty good money working for myself."

Susan still looked stiff and angry, but then the bristles faded. She gave Kelly another smug look.

"I've got to get ready for my date," she said. "So get the door for me when he comes, will you?" Susan headed upstairs.

Kelly took a bucket of soapy water, leather cleaner, and several rags out to her car. She cleaned the inside thoroughly, then hooked up a hose and washed the outside, buffing it dry, then adding a coat of finish-protecting polish.

She eyed the car critically, but could find nothing else that needed attention. She put the cleaning things away, gathered her purse and book bag from the couch, and carried them down the hall to her room.

The phone rang before Kelly could get her books out, and when Susan didn't answer it, Kelly did. Grease wandered out from the bathroom, stretching. She climbed up on Kelly's lap.

"This is Mrs. Rider," Kelly heard. "I'd like to speak to Kelly Frances."

The principal? Kelly thought. Did I do something? "Yes?" she asked cautiously, stroking her kitten.

"I was going over the student job directory forms, and I saw the one you filled out. Auto mechanics?"

"Right." Aren't mechanics included? she thought. Did I fill it out wrong?

"I asked around, Kelly. I hear you're pretty good. I wondered if you'd look at my car?"

"Oh, sure!" Kelly said, relieved. Grease nudged her arm, and she scratched the back of the cat's ears. "What's wrong with it?"

"It's making a noise. My husband said it seems to be coming from the transmission. Except he said revving the engine shouldn't make a transmission noise worse. And it does. Do you know about transmissions and things?"

"Sure," Kelly said. "I'll be glad to take a look at it, Mrs. Rider. I couldn't even guess what's wrong without hearing the noise myself. Are you driving it?"

"No. I left it downtown. I refuse to drive a car that sounds like it's ready to fall apart."

"I can pick it up then," Kelly offered. "If you'd like."

"I would like. Thanks. Why don't you stop by my office tomorrow for the keys?"

I could use a nice mechanical puzzle right about now, Kelly thought happily, hanging up the phone. It'll help take my mind off things. Like Danny. And finals. It won't interfere with studying. I'll still spend just as much time on my books. And I'm rationalizing. I feel just a little guilty taking on a job during finals week.

She grinned. I don't care, she thought. I want the job. It'll be a lot more fun than studying!

The doorbell rang. Susan's date, Kelly thought. I'm supposed to get that.

With her hand on the knob, she had a sudden recollection of Susan's smug look. And Kelly knew who stood on the other side of the door, knew from years of practice fitting Susan's little cues into a pattern.

24

6

"Hello, Danny," Kelly said calmly, pulling the door open. "Susan will be down in a minute."

"Kelly."

He nodded, grinning at her, his smile so familiar Kelly could almost feel it against her cheek as he whispered to her. His lean body, the one wave in the front of his dark hair, the glint in his brown eyes — it was all too recent to be a memory, but too firmly removed to be anything else.

"Come on in," Kelly said. Susan sure hit on a great way to get her digs in, she thought. And Danny has a perfect way to get back at me, too. He's got an excuse to keep calling and coming over.

Danny caught her arm as Kelly turned away from him. Her muscles contracted, her skin tingling even as she shook her arm loose.

"Let go," she said evenly.

"I've got something to say to you," Danny told her.

"I'm not interested."

"You're stubborn," Danny said. "I knew that.

But I thought you'd at least be fair and listen."

Slowly Kelly turned to face him. "Go ahead. But make it fast. I'm sure your date is just about ready."

"All I want is to have my say."

"You had your say already," Kelly told him. "As I recall, you said it with your fists."

"I said I was sorry!"

"Sorry gets dull after a while," Kelly said. "Repetitious. Your response is the same no matter what the problem is — you hit it. That's so predictable it's boring. Maybe one of these days you'll realize you can't solve anything with your fists. You can beat it to a pulp, but you can't solve it."

Danny's jaw clenched, his face reddening.

"Did you have your say?" Kelly said politely.

"I haven't even started," Danny said. He reached toward her, and before she could knock his hand away, he'd tipped the brim of her hat back.

It was a gesture so familiar Kelly had to exert iron control to keep from leaning forward to kiss him, to complete their ritual. I still care, she thought, confused. But I did the right thing breaking up with him. I know I did.

Danny knew what she was feeling — Kelly could see it both in his eyes and in his smile. She stepped backward, away from him.

"If you don't want me, I'm up for grabs," Danny said. "I can't help it if Susan is the one who grabbed first. I want you to know that. It's not my fault."

Kelly sighed. "Right," she said. "It never is."

Susan made her entrance, taking Danny's arm. "I'm ready," she said, smiling at him. She turned to Kelly. "Mom's working late all week, so you're on your own for dinner. 'Bye. Have fun studying."

Kelly watched them on their way to Danny's car, holding hands and talking to each other. My sister and my boyfriend, she thought.

Ex-boyfriend, she corrected herself firmly.

She settled down to study, plodding through her Geometry book chapter by chapter. She heard Danny's voice when he brought Susan home and was disgusted with herself when she realized she was trying to think of an excuse to wander out to the living room before he left.

She flipped to the next chapter and kept working.

Tuesday

7

She took it!

I can't believe she took it! It's mine!

Where did she hide it? What did she do with it? What will I do without it? I have to have it back. It's my blueprint. That's what he said. He said, "Take this. Let it work for you like it worked for me. It was my blueprint to success. It will do the same for you if you let it." See? I remember every word.

I need it! It's not for anyone else. Just me! He said so. "This is your secret. Just yours. There isn't room for very many winners in this world. But you can be one of them."

Why didn't she just leave it where it was? Does she know it's mine?

She can't. No one's ever seen it.

Till now.

Did she see me? She looked right at me. She must have seen me.

And she took my book. She'll know all the secrets!

I can't let her. I can't let her know my secrets. I can't let her have my book.

I am so stupid! I should have left it somewhere else. Somewhere safe. Then it wouldn't have fallen.

No, I'm not stupid. A stupid person couldn't have made a perfect plan like I did . . . couldn't have got the test. I got it. Maybe I should have been more careful, and maybe I should have put the panel back faster, but I'm not stupid. I'm a winner.

It's still a perfect plan. One problem didn't ruin my plan, and I won't let Kelly Frances ruin it, either.

8

Computer Literacy was Kelly's first class. Her stomach was an acid-filled pit by the time she got to school Tuesday, her hands stiff and cold. Their final exam was a forty-five-minute timed test, the material chosen by the teacher.

Kelly put her fingers on the keyboard and stared at the page she was supposed to type. The letters blurred. Her fingers felt too cold to move.

Relax! she ordered herself. She tried taking deep breaths and counting to ten slowly. I have to type something, she thought. Zero words per minute is about as low an F as I can get.

She remembered the teacher telling them not to say the letters or words to themselves as they worked. "Just look and type," she'd said. "Your mind interferes when it gets involved."

Kelly tried to see the letters and words without reading them, tried disconnecting her brain.

It didn't help.

My brain is already disengaged, she thought. My problem is I need to shift it into gear again. I wonder if it's the clutch on Mrs. Rider's car. I wonder if she pulls a trailer. That'll wear out a clutch. It could be a bracket on the pressure plate. A pivoting arm could have broken.

She disassembled the clutch assembly in her mind, examining it mentally, piece by piece, deciding which part was most likely to have broken, what noise each broken part would make. With her mind on the car, her fingers finally began working the keyboard.

"Time's up," the teacher said eventually. "Give your file your name and save it."

Kelly typed the save command, keyed in her name, and hit return, her relief that the test was over immediately replaced by dread of the next one.

She swallowed hard as she grabbed her books and joined the others in the hall, the acid pellets in her stomach reactivating themselves. Tests are too much like being under fire and having no protection, she thought. I don't like that pressure, I guess. I'm no good under pressure.

She smiled nervously at Tad Sedalia as he fell into step beside her in the hall. Senior class president, valedictorian, star of the baseball team, tall, blond, and good-looking, Tad was usually surrounded by a group of girls, enjoying it. He'd never joined her in the halls before.

"Ready for Geometry?" he asked.

"I was ready last night," Kelly told him, surprised at his attention, that he knew she had Geometry next. He wasn't in her class. He'd taken Geometry his freshman year and was in Calculus now. The only class he shared with Kelly was Spanish.

"What happened between last night and now?" Tad asked, grinning at her. "You can't forget overnight."

"I can," Kelly said. "I'm good at it. I seem to have a short circuit in my brain," she added. "Especially during finals."

"Performance anxiety," Ted said. "It's a killer. Hey, I heard about your car. I'm sorry. Egging a car is so juvenile."

"Thanks. It was pretty disgusting." Why is he walking with me? Kelly thought. Oh, the party. He wants to be sure I've heard about it.

"You know about my party, right?"

I'm good, Kelly thought. Psychic, even. "Yeah," she said. "It sounds like fun. Friday, your place. Right?"

"Right. Will you come?"

"Probably. If I'm still alive. I'm not expecting to survive five more finals."

"Do you have a date already?" Tad asked. "If you haven't told anyone else yes, I'd like to take you."

"You?" Kelly said, startled. The guy with the perfect life wants a date with me? she thought. Why?

" 'You?' " Tad repeated, sounding faintly insulted. "Yeah, me. Is there something wrong with me?"

"I didn't mean it like that," Kelly said, embarrassed. "Sorry. It's just that you surprised me. You've never been interested."

"Actually, I have been interested," Tad admitted, giving her an apologetic smile. "Who wouldn't be? I just wasn't interested in getting my face smashed. But since it looks like you and Danny have called it quits, I decided it was time to make my move. How about it?"

Kelly shrugged. "Sure," she said, still surprised. "I could do a lot worse than a date with a gorgeous hunk."

"I'm more than just another pretty face," Tad protested solemnly. "I'm smart, too. Columbus sailed the ocean blue in fourteen hundred and ninety-two. DC means either direct current or District of Columbia, depending which class you're in at the time it's mentioned. Two times two is four, two times four is eight — "

"Please, no math!" Kelly said, nodding at the door to the Geometry class. "I am two steps from math-saturation right now. I believe you. Gorgeous and smart. Such a deal."

"Can I pick you up early?" Tad asked. "I should be back home by the time people start arriving."

"I could drive," Kelly said. "I'll let you know. See you in Spanish."

"Well, I survived Geometry," Kelly told Talia at lunch. "I may not have passed, but I survived. You could be right. I might not die this week after all. You would not believe how many people I saw cheating."

"I know," Talia said. "It makes me mad. Eat, Jeffrey," she called to the table across from them.

"You need your vitamins. He's been kind of tense lately," she added in an undertone to Kelly. "The pressure's making him as crazy as y — oops."

"I know," Kelly said, grinning. "As crazy as me."

"Everybody's weird this week," Talia said. "It's like we're all walking around ready to explode."

"We're compressed," Kelly agreed.

"We're what?"

"Like tires," Kelly said. "With compressed air in them? If you just kept forcing air in, eventually the tires would explode."

"I get it, though it's not a very flattering comparison. Hmmm, I see Susan has a new friend."

Kelly made a face. "I keep telling myself it doesn't matter. I was done with him."

Talia grinned. "And one person's trash is obviously her sister's treasure. But why do they have to sit so close? To you, I mean. They're sitting close to each other, too, now that I mention closeness. But at least she's still in her own chair and not on his lap. Kelly, my dear, I think they're trying to egg you on. Oops. *Eggs* is a dirty word these days, right? But there are empty tables across the room."

"I guess I might not notice them if they sat over there," Kelly said. "I guess I'm supposed to be sure to notice."

Talia raised her eyebrows in question.

Kelly nodded. "Yes. I noticed. I also noticed that they switched seats in Spanish so they could sit together. Oh, Tee, remind me to go by Mrs. Rider's office today, will you? I'll forget."

"Are you in trouble? Why are you going to the

principal's . . . Kelly, you're not going to turn in the people you saw cheating!" Talia's voice rose.

There was sudden silence at the tables clustered near theirs, and Kelly glanced up to see what had caused it. She didn't see anything that would have caught everyone's attention.

Tad laughed. "I think they're all waiting for your answer, Kelly," he said. "Are you turning us all in?"

"I thought I was having a private conversation," Kelly said. "But I'll answer the question since everyone seems to want to know. I say, let he or she with the perfect conscience do the telling if any telling is going to be done. Come on, Talia. It's beautiful outside."

"And more private," Tad pointed out.

"Not if you and Jeff join us," Kelly invited. "You're welcome to."

"I'd rather it was just you and me, if you don't mind," Talia said quietly.

"Go ahead," Jeffrey told them. "I'll see you later, Talia."

Kelly decided Talia must have something important on her mind, but when they found a place outside, Talia just leaned back with her eyes closed, letting the sun warm her face. She didn't say a word.

9

"You okay, Talia?" Kelly finally asked.

Talia blinked, looking as if Kelly had startled her back from distant thoughts. "Sure," she said. "Hey, did I see the catch of the senior class walking through the halls in the arms of yours truly?"

"No arms," Kelly said. "Just walking."

"Yesterday you weren't all that impressed. As I recall, you thought your hat was more impressive than Tad, and now here you are, in the midst of a new romance. Were you planning to tell me or just let me guess? I shouldn't have to rely on the rumor mill, Kelly. I am your best friend. I should know about these things the instant they happen so I can be the one spreading stories, not the one who has to wait to hear the stories from others."

"You're current on the story," Kelly told her. "He asked me to his party. I said yes."

"As his *date?* Wonderful! But why? I mean, you're a great catch, Kelly, and I don't mean to be blunt, but I wouldn't have thought you were his type. He hasn't been known in the past for wild attractions to the dark, mechanical type. He broke up with that cheerleader person last month, and everyone's been taking bets on which other cheerleader person he'd ask out next. Actually, some people were betting on Susan. And he picked you!"

"I haven't exactly been picked," Kelly said. "I still might not be interested, you know. Besides, he only asked me out on one date. That is not picking. That is not a romance."

"It's the beginning," Talia insisted. "You were at least interested enough to say yes, right? And it's a mystery, besides. What happened in the perfect life of Tad Sedalia to rip him from his lifelong pursuit of the perfect cheerleader and thrust him in the path of . . ." Talia's voice trailed off and she stared at the ground. "Oh, never mind," she said.

"Talia," Kelly said.

"I'm fine. Just fine." Talia looked up at Kelly. She smiled. "You know what? You're going to be late for English again. That was the first bell."

"Oh, brother," Kelly said, standing. She gave Talia a hand up. "I hate sitting on that darned table." They started back across the athletic field. "You'd think I'd learn. Why don't I take my books to lunch so I don't have to go to my locker after lunch so I won't always be the last one to class and have to sit on that darned table?"

"Was that a question?" Talia asked.

"Rhetorical," Kelly said. "I don't expect an answer. It doesn't matter anymore, anyway. There aren't enough days left now to bother learning new tricks. I just wish they'd supply the classrooms with enough desks. That doesn't seem like too much to ask, does it?"

"Wouldn't think so," Talia said.

"They promised to order more desks. In fact, last time I checked, they said they'd put them on priority order."

"So where are they?" Talia asked.

"Still on priority order, no doubt. I'll bet they get them by next fall."

Talia shook her head. "See you in Chemistry," she said.

Kelly waved and went to her locker. Why did Tad ask me out? she wondered. Talia's right. I'm not his type. Is he my type? I'm not sure what my type is, after Danny . . . something smells funny. What smells funny?

She stopped in front of her locker, then stared without comprehension at the pale orange goo dripping from the vents.

What *is* it? she thought, opening the door.

10

"Yuck! That looks like that Cheez-Pleez stuff!"

Kelly looked at the people standing around, look-ing at her locker. Some faces were familiar, some weren't. They all looked disgusted, though, with wrinkled noses and expressions of distaste. Nobody looked guilty, or secretly gleeful, Kelly decided.

It looks like it's an hour or two old, Kelly thought. It's getting crusty where it's thin. I suppose it would be too much to hope that anyone saw anything.

"That's a sophomore trick," someone said. "I didn't expect to see it in the senior hall."

"They squirt it in through the vents," someone else said.

The final bell rang and the hall emptied, leaving Kelly staring at her locker, fuming.

This is absolutely a let's-get-Kelly attack, she thought, stalking to the rest room. It's not random vandalism. Egg my car and squirt fake cheese in my locker. She yanked out clumps of paper towels.

Who, though? she asked herself. Who's got a

grudge against me? What did I do? Who did I do it to?

Kelly grabbed the trash can and hauled it back to her locker, along with the towels. She swabbed and dabbed and scraped, then returned to the rest room for more paper towels, both wet and dry. English was half over before she trudged in and took her seat on the table in the back of the room.

"Sorry," she told the teacher. "I'll talk with you after class."

"You people think you can do whatever you want," the teacher said. "Four of you were late to class today. Just because you're *almost* out of here doesn't mean you can act like you've already graduated. You still have a few days left and I wish you'd remember it. Do you people think you could manage to get to class on time for three more days? Do you think you could manage to remember that you do still go to school?"

"What a crab!" someone hissed. "She's in a bad mood today."

The teacher glared around the room, then went on with the review. Kelly reached for her purse to get a pencil, but the purse wasn't on the table. She leaned down to look on the floor beneath the table. Her purse wasn't there, either.

She slid down from the table and headed for the door.

"Is something wrong, Miss Frances?"

Kelly sighed. "Yup," she said. She hurried out before she started crying in front of everyone.

She ran to the rest room she'd used while she'd

cleaned her locker. She dug through the trash, checked under the sinks.

It's not here, she thought. She leaned against the wall, discouraged. She wet a paper towel and held it on her eyes and then the back of her neck. After a while she felt cooled and a little calmer. She tried to remember when she'd last seen her purse.

I paid for lunch. I must have had it then. Did I leave it in the lunchroom?

She checked the senior hall, her locker, the lunchroom, then went outside to the place she and Talia had sat after lunch.

It's gone, she told herself. Someone took it. They egged my car, ruined my locker, and stole my purse. What is going on? Why me? What do they want?

11

The bell rang, signaling the end of fifth period. Kelly trudged back into the building, discouraged.

The walls and ceilings, the rows of lockers, the familiar faces all looked different, somehow.

It's not the same place I came to this morning, Kelly thought. It's changed. Now it's a place with an unknown, unseen enemy — waiting, hiding, planning another nasty trick to play on me.

She shivered. She pushed open the door to the office and asked to see Mrs. Rider.

"Kelly Frances? She's expecting you. Go on in."

The principal's office was lined with books and maps. The desk was huge, the dark wood polished, gleaming. It would be intimidating, Kelly decided, looking around, except for the vase of flowers, the bulletin board of student artwork, and Mrs. Rider. She's too cheery-looking to be intimidating.

"Hello, Mrs. Rider," Kelly said.

"Keys and an address," the principal said, handing them across the desk. "And the plate number, so you can make sure you have the right car before you get in. It wouldn't do to have someone call the police because you tried to start their car, thinking it was mine. It's a white Ford. And a question, Kelly. Your English teacher was just in."

"Oh," Kelly said. I should have known, she thought.

"Is there a problem?"

"Just some pranks," Kelly said. "It took a while to fix things up again. I'll apologize to Mrs. Beckman. I shouldn't have walked out."

"Especially not after being a half hour late."

Kelly nodded. "I know. But I had a reason."

"Pranks. Anything I should know about?"

"People are in high spirits," Kelly said. "Sometimes it gets out of hand. But I think I can take care of it with Mrs. Beckman. She was in a bad mood today, but she's pretty understanding. I'd rather handle it through her, if you don't mind."

Mrs. Rider smiled. "I'm the principal," she said. "You don't want to tell on anyone. I understand. Do it your way, Kelly. But remember, I'm here to help the students as well as the teachers. Do you know how long the car will take to fix?"

"Not until I look at it," Kelly said, grinning. "Are you in a rush? This is finals week."

"No real rush," Mrs. Rider said. "Except that I hate having to borrow a car."

"So, no rush but please hurry," Kelly said. "Got it. I'll call you when I know anything."

She was late to Phys Ed, but she had an admit from Mrs. Rider. The teacher looked surprised when Kelly handed her the pass. "I thought you seniors had given up getting passes," she said.

In Chemistry the teacher gave a review lecture, touching on the highlights from the first semester. "I'll cover the second semester tomorrow," she said. "Here's how the final is set up. It'll be open book."

Everyone cheered.

"Don't get too excited," she said. "It's still a hard test. And since it's open book, I'll expect absolute silence and I mean it. You walk in this class Thursday with your book ready, two pencils in hand, and your mouths shut."

"Two pencils?" Talia whispered.

"Two," the teacher said.

Talia looked surprised that she'd been overheard.

"You'll need two because no one is to leave his seat for any reason whatsoever. No one is to speak. Anyone who does either, flunks. Automatically. You are not even to raise your hand. I will not answer questions. You will take your test, then leave the room. That's it. See you tomorrow. We'll finish the review."

"Sheesh!" Kelly said as she and Talia gathered their things to leave. "I wonder if we flunk if we faint."

"Probably," Talia said. "At least, if you fall out of your seat when you faint. If you faint and stay in the chair, you'll probably be okay. I don't need a ride home, Kel. I've got a chance to spend a few hours with Jeffrey, for once. Seems like forever since we've had a real date. I'll be over later, though, if that's okay. To study Spanish. I'd love to work with Jeff, but we never seem to get anything serious done when we're together. Whenever he's got an audience he starts goofing around — so I'll be smart and study with you instead. You didn't suddenly decide to study with Susan, did you?"

"No," Kelly said. "I was hoping you'd come over. I'd appreciate the help reviewing. Have fun with Jeff." I was hoping she'd go with me to get Mrs. Rider's car, she thought, heading out into the hall. I haven't had a chance to talk with her since lunch. I didn't tell her about the squirt-cheese, or ask if she remembers seeing my purse. Oh, well. She might as well enjoy herself with Jeff instead of worrying about me.

Kelly got her Spanish book. Opening the locker made her angry all over again, and she slammed the door shut, glaring at the dents in the front panel.

Danny made the dents, she thought. Did he squirt the cheese?

She stalked toward the parking lot, trying to remember everything that had been in her purse. She'd have to replace the driver's license. The money was lost. Whoever took the purse would keep the money, even if the other things turned up later somewhere. Brush, comb, makeup — not too hard to replace. Checkbook. She'd have to call the bank to find out what to do about that.

At least I keep my keys in my pocket, she thought. I can still get home. But did I have a spare set in my purse?

"Kelly! 'Bye!"

She waved at friends, sidestepping as people drove out of their parking spaces, and then stopped, staring at her car.

Tad leaned against the T-bird's side, looking foolish and uncomfortable holding her purse.

12

"It was in the guys' locker room," he explained. "Nobody wanted to touch it. But I remembered you had one like it this morning so I looked inside. Your driver's license is in there. Cute picture."

"It's an awful picture," Kelly said. "But I'm very glad to have it back! I was furious, thinking someone had stolen it, and I'd have to replace everything. Is everything there?"

"I don't know," Tad said, grinning at her. "I don't usually carry purses, so I don't know what's supposed to be in them."

Kelly laughed, feeling relieved. She unzipped her purse, rifling through it. "That's odd," she said.

"What is?"

"The money's all here. Nobody steals a purse and leaves the money in it."

"Maybe they just wanted it to toss in the locker room," Tad suggested. "The guys are always doing that kind of thing."

"What kind of thing?"

"Oh, you know. Putting girls' stuff around. It's

a big joke to hang panty hose on someone's locker, or hide makeup in it."

"The makeup's here, too," Kelly said.

"Well, maybe I found it before whoever took it could get the makeup out," Tad said. "Is anything missing?"

Kelly checked more thoroughly. She frowned. Did I have a spare set of keys in here? she wondered. "I'm not sure," she told Tad. "I can't remember what all I had in it. But it looks like everything's here."

"Hmmm," Tad said, eyeing her. "I'm thinking about Friday night. Lovely ladies in swimsuits, burgers by the pool. Do you take your hat off to swim?"

"Of course I do."

"I'm looking forward to it," Ted said. "Am I picking you up?"

Kelly shrugged. "Why don't I drive?" she said. "Friday's going to be so crazy with final conferences and checkout and all that. We'll both be rushed all day, so if I drive, I can at least take my time getting ready."

"Okay. But next time we have a date, I drive. And we go together."

"Okay." Next time? Kelly thought. Talia will be delighted to hear he's planning a next time. "Thanks for my purse," she told him.

She drove to the address Mrs. Rider had given her, still wondering who had taken her purse, and why, and whether a spare set of keys had been in it. She parked in the restaurant lot next to a white

Ford, checked the license plate number. It matched.

Kelly unlocked the car and started it. Some noise! she thought. It's pretty loud. I'm not sure I've ever heard this precise noise before. It's familiar . . . but not quite right. She lifted the hood, peered underneath the car.

It's an odd noise, and definitely not the starter, she decided. I'd thought if the ring gear was loose, or if the starter itself was loose so it wasn't meshing right with the flywheel . . . but that's not the right noise.

Well, it's certainly drivable, at any rate. It's not falling apart right this minute.

She drove the car home, paying attention to the clutch as she operated it, the sound of the transmission shifting, the increase and decrease of the noise.

Well, it's not the transmission, she thought, parking the car in her work space between the garage and the house. The water pump's not leaking. It's vaguely similar to a water pump noise, but much, much louder. And coming from the transmission. Mr. Rider was right about that. But it's not a transmission noise.

She took a bus downtown to retrieve her car, puzzling about the noisy Ford. As soon as she was home again she went into the garage and put on her mechanic's coveralls, carried her tools from the T-bird's trunk and the garage, and set to work.

By the time Talia arrived to study Spanish, Kelly was even more puzzled.

"You look beautiful greasy," Talia teased.

"Thanks. Look. There's not a darned thing wrong with this. I mean, it's worn, but not broken. I was sure it had to be the pressure plate. But it's fine. The throw-out bearing is kind of bad, but not bad enough to make a noise like that."

"Then why are you smiling?" Talia asked. "You seem suspiciously happy about someone having a strange car problem."

"I'm having fun," Kelly admitted, grinning. "It's a puzzle. It's a mystery. I love solving mysteries."

"Now say all that again," Talia demanded. "In Spanish."

"In Spanish?"

"We have a Spanish final tomorrow, remember?"

Kelly made a face. "I was happily forgetting until you came along," she said.

"*Ahora,*" Talia said.

"Right now?" Kelly asked.

Talia nodded. "Wash up," she ordered. "*Ahora.*"

"Yeah, yeah," Kelly said, wiping the clutch pieces off with a rag. "I'm doing it now." She wrapped the pieces carefully and set them on the floor in the Ford's back seat. "I'd rather keep working here," she said hopefully. "You could ask me questions while I work. This is a good puzzle. I needed a good puzzle."

"I'd have thought the eggs were puzzle enough," Talia commented.

Kelly headed into the garage to use the waterless hand cleaner. "And the cheese. And my purse," she added.

"The what?" Talia scrambled up to follow.

Kelly explained, wiping her hands and forearms.

"That was your locker?" Talia asked. "I heard about the Cheez-Pleez, but I didn't hear whose locker it was. Wipe your face, too, Kelly. By your nose . . . and your brow. We should call you Grease instead of the cat."

"Say it in Spanish," Kelly told her, swabbing her face.

"No, seriously," Talia said. "What's going on? This is really mysterious."

"I have no idea," Kelly admitted. And thank heavens she didn't suggest Danny again, she thought. I'd hate to have to keep defending him. Could he have done it? "I'd say someone has a major grudge against me, wouldn't you? I mean, this is retaliation of some sort. Am I a rotten person?"

"No. Not that I've noticed. Your right ear, Kelly. And your face there, too."

Kelly swabbed at her ear. "I must be," she said. "Nobody vandalizes someone's car and locker and steals their purse for no reason. I did something. All I have to do is figure out what I did and who I did it to and then I'll . . . I'll know who's doing this and why."

"Kelly, if you were a rotten person I'd have noticed by now. Or someone would have told me. And then I'd have told you."

"Am I clean?" Kelly asked.

"Well, more or less."

"Let's go in then. I'll take a shower while you fix

me something to eat." Kelly stripped off her coveralls and rolled them up, dropping them on the workbench.

"You haven't eaten? It must be eight o'clock!"

"Is it? No wonder it's looking darkish out there. I was having too much fun to notice."

"Only you would call wallowing in grease fun," Talia said. "I'll go ahead of you and touch things, like doors, so you don't have to. I'll carry your hat for you, too."

"Talia, I do not wallow. Pigs wallow." Kelly followed Talia in the front door and down the hall. "I explore. I test. I check. I fix. I do not wallow."

Talia opened Kelly's bedroom door and stopped short. Kelly, close behind, walked right into her friend. "What?" she asked.

"Kelly!" Talia wailed. "Look at your room!"

13

Kelly edged around her and looked at her ruined bedroom. A wave of despair washed over her as she surveyed her clothes and books and stuffed animals strewn around. I can't stop them, she thought. Whoever it is just does whatever they want to do and I can't stop them.

Talia started spewing Spanish so fast that Kelly could only catch a word or two, here and there in the stream. "I'm saying your choice words for you," Talia explained, and started in again. She picked up an armload of clothes and started sorting and folding them. By the time Kelly recognized the same words again, she and Talia had cleared a path through the mess.

"You seem to have an impressive grasp of Spanish," Kelly said when Talia finally fell silent. "I don't think you need to study."

"Go shower," Talia told her. "I can handle things for a while here. I know where most of this stuff goes. You're just getting things greasy, anyway."

"I am raging," Kelly said. "The rest of the house looked fine when we came through. Someone was in my room. Just *my* room. I am ready to scream. Or cry. I would, too, except I can't decide which to do first." She wiped her eyes with the backs of her hands. "It's just so darned *mean*," she said. "It was a mean, pointless thing to do. They didn't take anything that I can see. Just trashed things. My things."

"It was mean," Talia agreed. "And pointless. It makes me furious, too. I'm boiling inside. But it doesn't help to boil. All that helps is cleaning up. And keeping your window locked, Kelly. You should never leave a ground-floor window unlocked."

"I'm real brainy about things like that," Kelly said bitterly. "It seems to me it was just yesterday that I had a problem with my car because I left it unlocked. You'd think I'd learn."

"Did you lock your car today?" Talia asked.

"I most certainly did."

"Then you learned. See? You're not hopeless, Kelly. A little slow maybe, but not hopeless."

Kelly tried to smile. She knew Talia was trying to cheer her up, but it wasn't working very well. Rooms are private, she thought. Personal. Full of personal things. It's a horrible feeling to see your room trashed. Your stuff scattered all over. It's awful to think of someone being in here without me even knowing it.

She shuddered and Talia hugged her, the hug

awkward as she avoided the worst of the grease in Kelly's hair.

Finally Kelly showered and when she returned to her room, it was nearly normal again.

"At least nothing was actually ruined," Talia said, forcing a smile. "You know, like things weren't torn up and there was no mustard squirted around or anything. The worst was the dirt from the plant and I think I salvaged most of it."

"Thanks, Tee," Kelly said, blinking back tears.

"Say it in Spanish."

"*Muchas gracias*, Talia."

"*De nada*. Why don't I fix you a sandwich while you finish up, and then we can hit the books for a little while."

I'm going to find the person who did this, Kelly thought, stacking her books back on the shelf. It's somebody mean. Someone with a petty, mean streak a mile wide, who also happens to hate me.

She kept working grimly.

"Your mom's home," Talia announced, carrying in a tray of sandwiches and fruit. "She says come say hi when you get a chance. I didn't tell her about this. Was I right?"

"Thanks," Kelly said. "No reason to get her all worried. Whatever is going on is aimed at me, not her. Not Susan."

"Susan's home, too. Danny brought her. Do you suppose they were studying Spanish?"

"Hmm," Kelly said.

"He looked to me like he was looking around for

you," Talia said. "He seemed pretty disappointed when he saw me and you weren't there, too."

"Hmm," Kelly said.

"Okay, I get the hint. I'll shut up about Danny."

"Say it in Spanish," Kelly said.

Wednesday

14

Where did she hide it? Where is it? I saw her put it in her book bag. I saw. But it wasn't there. It wasn't anywhere. And she went to the principal! Why? To tell on me, that's why.

What kind of game is she playing with me?

She acts so innocent. She doesn't say anything to me at all. Instead she's teasing and dropping hints and threatening me . . . talking about cheaters and saying she won't tell but she went to the principal.

This is nothing but a game for her. I need Winners. I need it to help me with my finals. I need it for all the decisions I have to make. It's important to me. It's my life, and she's playing with it! She said she wouldn't tell, but she did. They're going to come after me now and I don't know what to do. How can I know when she has my book?

Without Winners I can't think very well. I can't figure things out. I don't know what to do. I'm afraid. And they're going to come after me.

She doesn't want me to have it because she wants

to use it. I had to do something! So I did. I left her a surprise. But will it be enough? Will it stop her?

There's not room for very many winners in this world. I remember that. And I have to be one of them. She can't be. She stole my book and now she's told on me. I had to do something. She'll learn everything. Winners are in control. She'll be in control and I'll be nothing. I can't be nothing. I can't stand that. I can't stand it if they catch me.

I don't like being afraid. Let's see how she likes it.

15

Kelly had already taken the finals in her first three classes. The grades weren't posted yet but the classes were essentially over. Since there was no point in reviewing after the final, the teachers declared study hall and conferences.

Kelly was grateful for the extra study time. She and Talia hadn't had much time for Spanish after cleaning her room.

Kelly had gone to school early, apologized to her English teacher, and explained about the mess in her locker, the missing purse. "Once I realized I didn't have it, I had to go look for it," Kelly had said. "And I just couldn't stand there in front of the whole class and tell you what was going on. I just couldn't."

Mrs. Beckman had accepted the apology, but Kelly wasn't sure the teacher had believed her story. She'd seemed suspicious.

But then, *I'm* suspicious, Kelly thought. I'm suspicious of everybody. Just about. It's somebody who knows me. Someone who knows my locker, my car, my purse — even which room is mine. Who knows that? Talia. Danny. Susan. Who else? There has to be someone else. Almost everybody knows my car and my locker, and if I'm the one carrying a purse it's obvious to anyone looking that it's mine. But my room?

Kelly shivered, suddenly realizing that anybody could figure out which room was hers, just by watching the house. The idea of someone spying on her house was frightening.

She opened her locker slowly, expecting another unpleasant surprise. She jumped when someone called her name.

I'm a wreck, she thought. This is just like me. Put the pressure on and I fall apart. Who hates me? What did I do?

"Hey, Kelly."

She jumped again at Tad's hello.

"Are you okay?" Tad asked. "You looked spooked."

"Spanish final in three minutes," Kelly said. "Remember?"

"You're really serious about this performance anxiety stuff, aren't you?"

"No, just nervous about finals," Kelly told him.

"There's a trick I use sometimes," Tad said. "I pretend I'm taking the test for someone else. Sometimes that helps. It takes some of the pressure off. You could try that, or maybe pretend like it's a puzzle, like a rebus, that you're doing for fun."

"I'll try anything," Kelly said.

"Will you try going out for pizza with me to-night?"

"Tad, it's finals week! I've got to study!"

"You'll need a break from studying, I promise," Tad said. "And besides, you have to eat anyway. Would six be okay?"

"Six pizzas? That's too many."

"Six o'clock," he said, grinning. "We'll be back before your books even cool off."

"Okay," she told him. "We've got to get to class, Tad. We can't be late for a final."

She settled herself in her desk, glancing quickly around. Most of the faces looked anxious or nervous. Talia and Jeffrey quit whispering when the teacher stood. Susan looked smug, her usual expression. Tad gave Kelly a thumbs-up signal. Danny noticed and frowned.

"I've prepared an oral portion and a written portion for your final examination," the teacher said. "You will go to the lab ten at a time, for fifteen minutes. The rest of the time you'll be in here, working on the written section. You may leave your written tests on your desk, face down, while you go to the lab. Count off by three, please. That will give you your lab order. After that, no more talking."

Talia, Susan, and Tad headed off to the lab with the first group. Kelly would go in the third group. She wasn't as worried about the oral portion as the written, and it would have been nice to have a break doing the oral first to get her confidence level up before tackling the written section. Her hands were cold again, her stomach knotted. Her head hurt.

She stared at the test. The words swam.

No, she thought. This isn't rational. It isn't logical. I am a rational, logical person. I can do this. It's just like filling out a homework paper.

Wait. What did Tad say? Take the test for someone else. I'll pretend I'm taking it for Talia. This is just a homework paper of Talia's I'm doing for her.

She took a deep breath and stared at the first page again, reading the question. Oh, translate, she thought. Talia's good at translating. It says something about a moon. On a desert . . . landscape. And a . . . what? A . . . oh, it's a crack. In the earth. And a hand sticking up? Have I got that right? *Mano* is "hand," all right. What is this? Science fiction?

Slowly, intrigued, she was drawn into the story and worked steadily. Eventually the story switched to English and she had to translate to Spanish, which was harder, but she'd nearly finished the test when the aide summoned the number threes to the lab.

Kelly turned her paper over, almost lightheaded with relief, and left it on her desk. In the lab she put the headphones on, switched the machines on, and listened to the instructions. She corrected the sentences on the computer screen, answered the questions orally as the voice requested, and finally went back to class with the group as the bell rang, dismissing fourth period.

The tests had all been collected when the third group arrived, so Kelly grabbed her book bag, made certain she still had her purse, and headed for lunch.

Talia had saved her a seat. Kelly bought a lunch and joined her friend.

"Hey," she told Talia. "I think I did all right! I was actually able to write. I held my pencil and everything! The test made sense! I'm so glad it's over. How did you do?"

"Not bad, I think," Talia said. "I'm a little worried about Jeff, though. Every time I looked over he was staring off into space."

"You were only in class together the last fifteen minutes," Kelly pointed out. "You were a one. He was a two. Maybe he finished up fast. He's pretty good, isn't he?"

"I suppose," Talia said. "There's not much we can do about it afterward, anyway. That's the thing about finals. They're pretty final, all right. I'm glad you did okay. What happened? Is this a permanent change? Instant cure? No more nerves?"

Kelly took a deep breath and let it out slowly, trying to put herself into tomorrow, into her Chemistry and English finals. The thought of English set her stomach churning again and she pushed her tray aside.

"I was hoping," she said, making a face. "But I guess the big test is tomorrow. English. That's the real test."

16

Kelly stopped by Mrs. Rider's office before going home. She explained that the clutch assembly was worn, though it hadn't turned out to be the cause of the noise.

"It's not really any problem to pull the transmission," Kelly said. "So replacing the clutch in a Ford is no big deal. I just figured as long as I had it apart, you might want to save a repair bill later and have me replace it now. It could still work fine for another year, or, depending how you drive and whether you pull a trailer, it could go bad in a few months. It's up to you."

"What would you do if it was your car?" Mrs. Rider asked.

Kelly smiled. "I'd run it a while longer and then tear it down for fun and see how much it had worn."

Mrs. Rider laughed. "Replace it," she said. "I have no intention of tearing anything on that car down for fun or for any other reason. You might as well do it while it's apart. Do you need a check for parts?"

"I have accounts at a couple of parts shops," Kelly said. "It's no problem to run a tab. Clutches are pretty cheap, actually. It's the labor that adds up, and I'll only charge half price for the job since I had the car apart anyway. I'll give you a list of other things that need to be fixed, watched, or replaced, too."

"Is it in bad shape?"

Kelly shook her head. "Looks pretty good, actually."

"That's a relief. Thanks, Kelly. Every time a car makes a new noise I panic. Like the bottom of my heart drops right into my stomach. I feel like I'm suddenly doomed. And it's so silly. A noise doesn't mean instant disaster, but I panic anyway. It isn't rational."

Kelly laughed. "I think noises are interesting," she said. "I love figuring out what's causing them and why that problem creates that particular noise. They don't scare me at all. But instant disaster describes exactly how I feel about taking tests! Especially finals. I'll be glad when this week is over!"

Kelly scooted out from under the Ford, the wheels on her creeper scraping against the concrete.

"It's not six," she said. "It can't be."

"Five till," Tad told her. "I'm early. Looks like you're going to be late."

"It's not as bad as it looks," Kelly said, grinning at him. "I'm just meditating."

"You're what?"

"Thinking. Looking. I'm not really touching anything."

"Oh," Tad said, eyeing her hands, then her greasy coveralls. "I'd hate to see you touch anything, then."

Kelly raised her eyebrows and Tad laughed. "I mean it," he said. "I never thought I'd tell a girl this, but Kelly Frances, keep your hands off me."

Kelly stood up and unzipped her coveralls. She led the way into the garage and washed her hands with Goop, then with soap in a basin of water she'd brought out. She peeled off the coveralls, pulled the cap from her head and stood in front of Tad, clean and dressed in jeans and a blouse. She turned in a circle.

"See?" she said. "Not a speck of grease on me. Six o'clock and I'm ready." She put her derby hat back on.

"I'm impressed," he said, nodding his approval. "Can I take back what I said?"

"Nope," she told him. She closed and locked the garage. "I'm keeping my hands to myself, as ordered. I'm very obedient."

"Please?" He opened the car door for her.

"I'll think about it," Kelly promised.

"I like thoughtful people," Tad said, starting the car. "As new evidence appears, a person must be ready to think about his or her stance on issues and reevaluate. I was. As your hands got cleaner, I was more and more willing to reevaluate. . . ."

"I get the picture," Kelly said, laughing. "I will try to keep an open mind."

"Good. Is Shepp's okay?"

"Perfect."

After a brief pause, Tad said, "Susan is your sister?"

"Yeah, why?"

"You two are very different!" Tad said. "Even with the same last name, I didn't realize you were related. She was watching us as we left. Out the front window."

"Do you know her?" Kelly asked.

"Well, kind of. She's in Spanish, of course. And she's a cheerleader. She cheers at the JV games, not mine, but of course I've seen her around."

Talia said Susan was more his type, Kelly thought. Is that why he asked me out? To meet Susan? But that's dumb. He could meet her himself, any time he wanted to. "Do you want me to introduce you?" she asked.

"Not really," Tad said. "It's not hard to meet cheerleaders. Especially if you're on any of the teams. It's much harder to meet female mechanics."

"I'm not hard to meet," Kelly said. "Walk up. Say hi. Which is pretty much what you did."

"Yeah." Tad looked thoughtful, and Kelly wondered, again, why he had asked her out. Is it because he wanted to see what a female mechanic is like? Because that's weird?

I could just ask him, I guess, she thought. But she couldn't think of a way to do it that didn't sound stupid. The silence lasted until they were at Shepp's, seated. Then they argued good-naturedly about the perfect pizza, finally ordering one with thick crust, extra cheese, and no bell peppers.

He's different from Danny, she thought, watching him as he poured Coke from the pitcher into their glasses. More relaxed. Danny's always kind of hyper, like he's so full of nervous energy he can hardly keep it inside. Tad's more low-key. But that makes it harder to figure out what he's thinking, too. What is he thinking? Why did he ask me out?

"What are you doing this summer?" he asked.

Kelly shrugged. "Working on cars," she said. "But I haven't decided where." She explained about her father's job offer. "It could be kind of fun," she said. "Traveling with the race cars. Working on them. They're pretty exciting machines."

"I think it sounds great!" Tad said.

"Not great," Kelly told him. "First of all, the other mechanics will be really good. They'll all be senior to me, too. I'm not sure they'll even let me touch the cars. Second, I'm not exactly the nomad type. Dad's happy with a country-western song and any old shelter from the storm. I like my privacy, my comfort, and a little predictability. I also like being my own boss. Besides . . ."

She paused. She'd been going to say that it would make her sister jealous, but that seemed too personal to mention to someone she barely knew.

"I'd miss everybody," she finished. "What are you doing this summer?"

"I haven't decided, either," Tad said. "I've got

college in the fall, so it seems like I ought to party all summer long. Kind of as preparation for four years of grind."

"I can't imagine a ninety-day party."

"Oh, I can," Tad said, grinning. "My sister . . . she lives in Texas. She as much as promised me a nonstop party if I'd spend the summer with her and her husband. Mom wants me to go to Europe with her, but she's going to shop. I'm not sure I want to spend my summer in little boutiques in Paris."

"You'd be able to do some sightseeing, too, I'm sure," Kelly said. "It sounds great to me." Europe? she thought. He doesn't live in my world! I don't live in a world where I have to choose between going to Europe or to a ninety-day party in Texas! I've got tuition money to earn! The only question I've got is where I'll be earning it, not whether.

They talked about their finals and mutual friends, and on the way back to Kelly's, discussed Tad's party. Kelly couldn't quite relax. She didn't feel entirely comfortable with Tad, with his expensive car and perfect manners. His fingernails have never felt the touch of grease, she thought, sourly amused. He's probably never even seen a spark plug or a wrench, or changed a tire. He probably gets the chauffeur to do it for him.

That's not fair, she told herself. He's driving himself. He doesn't have a chauffeur. He doesn't even have a car phone.

"What's it like, being a mechanic?" Tad asked as they stopped at her drive.

"Greasy," Kelly said, frowning. What kind of

question is that? she thought. There's nothing mysterious about mechanics. He thinks I'm odd.

"Yeah, grease and nuts and bolts," Ted said. "But what makes you like it?"

Is he making fun of me, or does he really want to know? she wondered. "I've always been fascinated with how things work," she said finally. "All these little pieces, like a puzzle. Only when they're all put together in a machine, they make a lot more of something than a puzzle does. Puzzles are kind of lifeless. Machines are useful, functional things."

"Did you and your father do a lot of things together?"

Kelly thought Tad sounded odd, somehow, and she looked at him. But she couldn't read his face. She thought of his father at the ball game, shouting, critical. "I guess we did," she said. "He's very mechanical. Every time I'd get in trouble with Mom for taking her things apart, he'd help me get them back together. And then he'd take me out and have me help him fix something on one of the cars. I could do a basic tune-up by the time I was eight."

"I can't even do one now," Tad admitted.

"Sure you could, if you tried. They're easy."

They both turned around at the sound of a car driving up behind them.

"Hmm," Ted said.

"Yeah," Kelly agreed.

Danny and Susan had driven up, parking right behind them. As Kelly and Tad watched, Danny pulled Susan close to kiss her. Kelly turned away.

She could almost feel the kiss. She closed her eyes but it didn't shut out her memories.

"You went together a long time," Tad said quietly.

"Almost three years," Kelly said. She looked at Tad. "Do you mind walking me to the door?"

"Not at all. I was enjoying talking with you, but I guess we can talk Friday." He got out, and opened her car door. "I'd love to hear more about curious Kelly, age six, getting in trouble for taking things apart. I barely dared touch anything in my house, and I wouldn't have dreamed of taking anything apart!"

Kelly grinned at him, ignoring the car behind them as she and Tad headed for the front door. "You know those little wires in a toaster?" she asked. "The ones the bread rests against when it's toasting? They never do go back in right, once you take them apart."

"Never?"

"Uh-uh. Never. At least not that Dad nor I could figure out. We had to buy a new toaster. That's when I decided against a career in small-appliance repair. As a matter of fact, that's about the time my dad got me my first car. I was ten."

"You had a car when you were ten years old?"

"Yeah." Kelly laughed, remembering. "A 1954 Chevy. It was a goner. I never did get it running. I figured out later that Dad got it for me just so I'd have something to take apart and would leave

Mom's hair dryers and washing machines and vacuums alone. But at the time, I was convinced I could get that car working eventually. Thanks, Tad. For the pizza and the rescue."

"You didn't need anyone to rescue you," Tad said. "You've got more class than those two, Kelly. Any day. See you tomorrow."

What did he want? Kelly asked herself, getting ready for bed. Is it a sociological experiment? The European vacation guy and the female mechanic? Is he checking out the lower class to see how they live?

That's not fair, she decided, brushing her teeth. He's not a snob. He was very nice. Polite. And he invited the whole senior class to his end-of-finals party, not just the cheerleaders and jocks. And it's not the first time he's done it, either, even if it is the first time I decided to go to one of his parties. He's never been elitist about inviting people over. I have to admit he's nice. I like him fine.

But what does he want with me?

She looked at herself in the bathroom mirror. I'm short and strong, she thought. And I'm okay-looking. Not like Susan, maybe, but pretty enough. But still, Talia was right. I'm not his type. So what does he want with me?

She reached down absently to pet Grease, who was winding herself around Kelly's legs, purring loudly. "Got any ideas?" she asked the cat.

She fell asleep still wondering, fell into the midst of a dream that seemed to have been going on long before she entered it.

17

Hands that belonged to unseen beings dressed her in black robes, urged her along a dim passageway, guided her into a chair in front of a polished desk.

Kelly leaned forward, peering over the edge of the desk. Below her, looking small, hands cuffed behind their backs, stood Danny and Susan, Jeff and Talia, and Tad, alone. I have to pass judgment, Kelly realized. Guilty or not guilty. But of what?

"What are the charges?" she asked.

"You have to charge us," Susan said. "What am I accused of?"

"Taking Danny," Kelly said.

Susan laughed. She looked beautiful, even in the faded green jail clothing. "What is this, a trap?" Susan asked. "There was no taking. Danny came of his own free will."

She's right, Kelly thought.

"You didn't want me," Danny said. "You threw me away. I'm not garbage, Kelly. I didn't like being thrown away. It wasn't a nice thing to do."

"What am I accused of?" Talia asked, crying.

Kelly felt an enormous sadness at Talia's tears. "Don't cry," she said. "You didn't do anything."

"Then why am I here?" Talia asked. "I don't know what's going on. I hate it when I don't know what's going on."

"Why am I here?" Tad asked. "It hardly seems fair. You're up there deciding our lives, you know."

Kelly didn't know what to say to them, and suddenly she was the one wearing jail clothes, except they were coveralls. Faded green mechanic's coveralls.

"Why?" Tad demanded, looming over her.

"Why?" Jeffrey echoed. "You may speak in your own defense. You have the right to defend yourself."

They all loomed over her, huge and demanding. Kelly felt compelled to answer, now that she was the one in handcuffs. She had to answer. It was the rules. "You were examining me," she told Tad. "Like I was an alien or something."

Suddenly they were all chanting her name and pounding on the desk. "Kelly! Kelly!" Pound, pound.

What do they want? she wondered, confused. Her head hurt. Why is it so smoky in here?

Then Kelly realized she was wide awake. She wasn't dreaming.

18

"Kelly! Kelly!"

I'm awake, she thought. I can't breathe.

"Kelly? Are you all right? What's going on in there?" Susan called.

Kelly couldn't answer.

The door opened, and Susan poked her head in. "Good grief!" she shouted. She flipped the light on, then disappeared, returning quickly with the bathroom wastebasket.

Kelly just watched, feeling nauseated and numb. She didn't realize her bedroom trash can was on fire until she saw the flames die under the deluge of water Susan dumped from the bathroom wastebasket. It didn't occur to her to open the window until Susan threw it open, and the breeze started clearing away the smoke and fumes.

"Your trash can was on fire!" Susan said, horrified. She covered her mouth with her hands. "How awful! Are you okay? I thought I smelled smoke, but I didn't think it was this bad! The door has a tight fit. Kelly, are you all right?"

"I think so," Kelly managed. Her throat felt acrid and her head was pounding, but the light-headedness had eased as the smoke cleared.

"The smell was awful!" Susan said, her voice shaky. "What happened?"

Kelly sat up slowly, experimentally. She didn't faint, and the movement didn't make her head hurt worse. "Was the window latched?" she asked.

"What?"

"When you opened the window, was it locked?"

"I . . . I don't think so," Susan said. "I think . . . I just pushed it up. I'm not sure, but I don't remember unlocking it. Maybe I didn't notice."

Kelly bit her lower lip, trying to remember if she'd locked her window. A tomcat yowled outside and Susan jumped, then ran to close the window again.

"Lock it, please," Kelly said.

"Your trash can melted into the carpet!" Susan said, her voice still shaking.

"It's okay," Kelly said. "I'm alive."

Susan looked even more horrified. "You couldn't have died," she said.

"Plastic fumes are toxic," Kelly told her. "The fire was melting the carpet. Nylon fumes are toxic, too. You saved my life, Suze. Corny, maybe. But true. Thanks."

Susan's look of horror didn't fade. She looked slowly around the room, then at Kelly, her eyes dark and frightened.

"It's okay," Kelly said again. "I didn't die, thanks

to you. I've just got a massive headache, and Tylenol will take care of that."

"I'm going to be sick," Susan said, clapping her hand over her mouth. She ran for the bathroom.

Kelly got up slowly, took the bathroom wastebasket, and followed Susan. She felt a little dizzy, but even that eased as she stood in the hall. In a few minutes Susan emerged from the bathroom, looking pale, her face blotchy and puffy.

"You okay?" Kelly asked.

Susan nodded.

"Susan . . . I . . ." Kelly's words faltered. How do you thank someone for your life? she wondered. Especially someone you don't get along with?

"Don't say a word about it, ever again," Susan said. "Okay? It scared me and it made me sick and I don't want to talk about it or think about it. Ever."

"Okay," Kelly said slowly. "But . . ."

Susan turned away, hurrying upstairs.

Kelly set the trash can back where it belonged, then went back into her room and stared at the molten lump of plastic and carpet. She nudged it with her toe, but it didn't budge. The carpet around the wastebasket had blackened into melted, ropy blobs.

The reality of the situation hit Kelly and she collapsed onto her bed, shaking. I could have died! she thought. Really died! Someone tried to kill me.

After a long time the shakes lessened and she tried to think. Did someone really try to kill me? Could it have been an accident? Things don't just catch on fire. Something has to ignite them. Did I have any oily rags in here? No. I never work in here. Was there anything flammable in my room? Lighter fluid? Turpentine? Gasoline? Cleaning fluids? Anything?

I don't think so. Could I have spilled gas on something I was wearing? Maybe. But were any of my clothes near the trash can?

Should I call the police?

What for? There's nothing left of the trash can. No clues. Susan opened the window. If there were any fingerprints, she messed them up. If I call the police, they'll wake Mom and scare her half to death. And they'll ask me thousands of questions and I'll miss my finals and either the police will think I'm crazy or they'll poke around forever and then not find anything anyway.

She sat and stared out the window until the sun came up, trying to find some kind of sense in the attacks that had suddenly become too frightening.

It's not just vandalism anymore, she thought. I can't think why someone would want to hurt me. But someone does. Someone is serious. Someone hates me. If I don't know why, can I figure out who? How would I go about figuring who? There's no starting place.

This all started Monday with the eggs. So what happened Monday? I filled out the job forms. I found that little book. Oh, I forgot to ask around about it. Talia and I watched the team practice. Tad's father was there. Dad called and asked Susan to tell me about the job. Susan and Danny had a date.

Mrs. Rider called. I argued with Danny. I studied.

She sighed. Nothing seemed connected. Nothing pointed to any person or reason.

Clues, she thought, turning on the water for a shower. I need clues. Eggs and cheese. Somebody who's obsessed with food? Vandalism. My room, my car, my locker. Vandals are childish or angry. So who's childish? Who do I know who gets very angry about things? Danny, of course. But he's not a vandal. My purse. The fire. It's someone who's getting more serious. This *is* getting serious.

"But *who* is it?" she shouted. The spatting and drumming of the water was her only answer.

Thursday

19

Doesn't she understand? My whole life is on the line. If I'm not a winner, I might as well be dead.

I can't stand not knowing what's going on. She went to the principal, but nothing happened. They didn't come and get me yesterday. Will they get me today? They aren't going to just forget the whole thing. They must be planning something.

But what? They must be planning to trap me. Some place and some time when I'm not expecting it, when they can take me by surprise. They're setting out traps and any minute . . . any second I could get caught in one. I'm afraid. Is she afraid now, too?

I'm being hunted, and she is the one hunting me. I had to do it. And if I have to do more, I will.

I just can't stand it. I can't sit here and wait for her to ruin my life. I do have to do more. I haven't stopped her yet.

If she flunks, she won't graduate. She'll be stuck here and I'll be gone. Safe.

I have the right to defend myself.

She made the rules, but I can play by them, too. She thinks she's the hunter, so sly and innocent-acting. She thinks I'm going to be easy to catch, and she can take her time, playing with me first, teasing. Then she'll pounce, just when I think I'm safest.

Well, she's finding out. Sometimes the hunter turns out to be the hunted. I can lay traps, too.

20

Thursday dawned clear and shining, the blue of the sky almost too deep to be real. Kelly could feel that yearning pull of spring and freedom, the pull to skip the day's responsibilities and go lie in the sun, dangle her feet in a stream, stretch out in a meadow and watch the wind tease the wildflowers.

The yearning added an undertone to her distraction, made her feel wistful, but the fact that she was heading to school to take final exams barely registered in her mind. Her thoughts were only of the fire in the night, the mysterious person who was after her, and the fear that the person wasn't finished with her yet.

I played right into their hands, leaving my window unlocked, she thought. Unless . . . unless my spare keys were in my purse!

How could I be so stupid? What if someone has a set of keys to my house and my car? Locking my window won't be enough.

The thought was so chilling that it colored the morning. Kelly stumbled through the halls, almost in a daze except that she was suspiciously alert. She studied everything everyone did or said, watching for guilty looks, for knowing glances, for leading questions that weren't as innocent as they might seem.

"Hi," Tad said in the hall before first hour. "Did you sleep well?"

"Why do you ask?" Kelly asked quickly. How does he know I didn't sleep? she thought. Could he . . .?

Tad looked surprised. "You've been so worried about the tests," he said. "You know? All that performance anxiety? And you look worn out, like you haven't been sleeping well. I have to admit I did a little tossing and turning myself. I wonder if anyone's getting enough sleep this week."

"I'm okay, thanks," Kelly said, relieved.

"Did you like my trick?" he asked.

"What trick?" she asked, alert and suspicious all over again.

Tad looked a trifle annoyed, then sighed. "It's a rough week," he muttered.

"What trick?" Kelly repeated. "Oh." She felt stupid as she figured it out, and made a face, shaking her head. "Taking the test as if I were taking it for someone else," she said. "It helped a lot, Tad. Thanks."

"Any time," he said. "Glad to help. You know, I've never been so glad it's almost Friday in all my life. Everybody's so weird!"

I'll say! Kelly thought.

At lunch she wandered outside with her food and

her English and Chemistry books, planning to study a little after she ate. But when she finished her food, she sprawled out on the lawn, letting the sun soak into her tense muscles.

This is it for finals, she thought. English and Chemistry today. All I have tomorrow is the Phys Ed test.

But her finals seemed almost as distant as the sun, less important than the hypnotic warmth on her back and the one question that beat in her mind.

Who?

Who is it, and who can I trust? Can I trust anyone? It could be anyone. But not Talia. I can trust her. I can't go around being suspicious of everybody. The only thing that's changed since Monday is Tad. He's suddenly interested. Is that suspicious? Nothing else is different. I don't want to think any more.

"There you are, lazy," came Talia's voice. "Tad said you didn't sleep last night and you were zonked out on the lawn. Are you sleeping?"

Kelly rolled over and pulled her hat brim down to shield her eyes from the sun, looking up at Talia. "Not anymore," she said. I guess I did doze off, she thought, surprised. I'm tired after last night.

"Are you okay?" Talia asked.

"Why?" Kelly demanded, suddenly alert again. Not Talia, she thought. Not her.

"Tad said you weren't tracking real well. And looked tired. He seemed worried."

"How well do we know him, anyway?" Kelly

asked. "Sit down, or else stand so you block the sun, will you?"

Talia sat with her back to the sun, looking thoughtful. Kelly moved so she was facing the same direction, tipping her hat brim up now that the sun was no longer in her eyes.

"Everybody knows Tad," Talia said. "I guess I don't understand the question."

"He's popular," Kelly said. "So of course everybody knows him. He comes from a well-off family. He's smart. He's everybody's favorite athlete. But what does anyone know about him? Like old stories, things that might give a clue to his personality. You know, like Jeffrey hunting up a pig to turn loose during that boring assembly. That tells a lot about Jeffrey. Do you know anything about Tad?"

Talia frowned. "You don't think he egged your car, and did all those things, do you? Just because he's the one who found your purse?"

"No, not really," Kelly said. "I'm just curious about him. After all, he seems to have a sudden, unexplained interest in me, and even you said it was weird. I'd like to know a little bit about who he is."

"Well, hmmm. He's lived here a long time. I remember him from elementary school, even. He's just Tad. I guess he's been involved in all the usual stuff all along. When Jeffrey thought up the idea of drilling a hole into the girls' locker room and drilled into the coach's office instead, Tad was in the group. That was in junior high."

Hmm, Kelly thought. Vandalism.

"No one's ever had anything particularly bad to say about him. He's been in his share of fights and stuff, but never seems to pick them. I guess he's just a regular kind of person, Kelly."

"How about lighting fires or cheating on tests?" Kelly asked. "Any rumors?"

Talia shook her head. "I told you. He has the perfect life. Rich, good-looking, smart, and popular."

"Then there *has* to be something wrong with him," Kelly said. "Nobody's that perfect."

"Did something else happen to you?" Talia asked.

"Why?" Kelly hated her suspicions, but couldn't seem to stop them.

"You seem determined to find out that Tad's a rat," Talia said, eyeing Kelly. "Like you want him to be. You didn't want him to be the last time we discussed him. So I figured maybe something else happened."

"No," Kelly said. "Nothing happened." Susan won't tell anyone about the fire, she thought. She was too upset. So I won't say anything, either. And then, if someone knows . . . She didn't want to finish the thought.

"And you're fine?"

"Fine," Kelly said.

"Good. I wish I was."

"What's wrong?" Kelly asked.

Talia sighed. She stared at the ground. "Nothing, really," she said. "It's just that everything's ending, you know? We're not kids anymore, Kelly. We're headed off into the world. That was exciting, until it all got so real. I'm not so sure I'm ready to be on my own."

"You know what I heard?" Kelly asked. "I heard that in school we get the lessons first, and then take the tests. But in life, we get hit with the tests first, and then have to figure out the lessons afterward."

"That's it, exactly," Talia said, giving Kelly an uncertain smile. "You do understand. I knew you would. I'm not ready to go out and face life's tests. I'd rather have more time to study first. I still need the lessons first. I'm not ready for all those decisions."

"Hey, you make decisions all the time," Kelly told her. "From little things like choosing what to wear and pack for lunch, to things like whether to go out with Jeff or stay home and study. You've had a lot more practice than you think, and you've done a pretty good job. College and marriage and moving away from home may be bigger choices, but they require the same skills as the little decisions. You can handle it."

"Sometimes I get in over my head," Talia said. "Do one stupid thing after another. Then I don't know how to stop the whole thing. Like a roller coaster ride. You get on, you stay on till the ride stops. Only this one isn't stopping."

Kelly felt chilled. Talia is trying to tell me something, she thought. In fact, it sounds like Talia has a secret that she wants me to ask her about. And keep asking until she tells me. And I don't want to know it. No matter what she's saying, no matter what it sounds like, I don't believe that Talia would ever do anything to hurt me.

"I don't know what you mean," Kelly finally said.

"Oh, that's all right," Talia told her. "I don't mean anything. I'm just running off at the mouth, like I always do. Come on, it's time to go back in."

Kelly was the last one to English again. She nodded to friends as she passed through the aisles and tossed her books onto the table. She took a deep breath and let it out slowly. Why did Talia have to act so mysterious? she thought. I don't want it to be Talia, but no one else has acted strangely, lately. Except maybe Tad, for asking me out.

She stood with her back to the table, then leaned on her hands and hopped up to sit.

The table collapsed under her weight.

21

The table legs scooted out sideways on either end, the stacks of books tumbling forward, some thunking off of Kelly's head and shoulders before skittering across the floor.

Kelly felt the books hit, felt a painful scraping on her back as she slid to the floor, felt the thump as her head bounced back against the table, her hat flying off. Mostly, she felt rage and fear and betrayal.

Even here! she thought. Even in a classroom with thirty other people. I'm not safe anywhere!

Then she heard the noise — people screaming and asking if she was all right — and saw the faces, shocked, mouths open or covered with hands, eyes alarmed and concerned.

"I want a desk," Kelly said.

"I think you should go to the nurse's office," Mrs. Beckman said.

"I'm okay," Kelly told her, getting up slowly. Her back stung, but she could tell it was just a skin scrape, not a sprain or spinal injury. Her head and shoulders felt pummeled from the books that had tumbled over her, but it wasn't the kind of problem that would be helped by a visit to the nurse.

Kelly retrieved her hat, then insisted on helping straighten the rubble of books and set the table against the wall, out of the way. As she helped, she looked for the screws that should have held the legs to the underside of the table top.

There were two I-shaped steel plates, with two legs welded onto each plate, one at each end of the I. The plates were then screwed onto the table so there was an I on each end, running across the short way. Kelly counted twelve screw holes in each plate.

There should be twenty-four screws, then, Kelly thought.

She found four.

Taking finals is getting dangerous, she thought. Being in school is dangerous. I knew I didn't like taking tests.

"We still have a final to take," Mrs. Beckman announced. "Kelly, you may sit at my desk. We no longer have the full class period so you'd better get started."

She handed out the exams.

Some of the screws could have rolled away, Kelly thought. But not all of them. If there were only two screws in each leg all along it wouldn't have held. No matter how many screws there were, if they'd worked themselves gradually loose the table would have been wobbly, and I'd have felt it. The table was sturdy. It's been sturdy all year. Including yesterday. It was fine yesterday. Somebody took the screws out. They just left enough screws in to hold it together till I sat on it.

She looked at the test. Question number one said to explain how, in at least one of the stories they'd studied, the author had used the antagonist to represent the dark side of the protagonist.

She shivered. It was chilling to know that somehow, someone had managed to attack her in English class.

Antagonist, she thought, scribbling quickly. The person who is working against the protagonist or hero. I've got one of those in my life. It makes me feel weak and ineffective. Jumpy. Frightened. And suspicious. Is that how Jason felt getting ready to launch the Argo? No, he could see his antagonists. He always had a definite enemy he could face and fight. Not this shadowy threat that lurks around, waiting and planning so I never know when to watch out.

Jason had it easier. It's easier to fight a known enemy than a sneaky, hidden one you never see. Was he ever afraid? He should have been, but he never looked inside to see what was really going on. He just kept fighting. He didn't want to pull any fears out and look at them because then he might have to admit they were real, so he fought the antagonists instead! Do I represent someone's hidden fears? Is someone fighting me instead of looking inside?

Kelly finished writing and read the second question. The story it named was *Frankenstein*, which they'd read at the beginning of the year. Kelly hadn't liked the story. She thought it was too sad, and she was ready to skip the question until she focused on the word *danger*. I can relate to danger, she thought.

She reread the question. "Discuss the nature of Dr. Frankenstein's danger."

It's a stupid question, Kelly thought. The poor monster was the one in danger. Frankenstein just kept running away from him — escaping danger. But . . . it's the same thing again. Frankenstein's real danger was hidden. The monster was a physical symbol of danger, but the real problem was the creator's refusal to accept responsibility for his creation. That was his hidden danger. My danger is both physical and hidden, too. I'd be glad to accept responsibility for it if I could just find it!

She shivered again and started writing, her thoughts too rapid for her pen to keep up with.

She looked up, astounded, when the bell rang. She looked back at her paper. She hadn't quite finished the last question, but had answered everything. She handed in her test.

"Are you going to have the nurse check you out?" Mrs. Beckman asked.

Kelly shook her head. "I'm fine," she said. "Really." She gathered her things and headed for Phys Ed, which turned out to be an outdoor study hall for the half of the class that wasn't testing today. Kelly's test was the next day so she grabbed her books and found a half-shaded place outside.

She took off her hat and stretched out, resting. She kept telling herself she should be reviewing Chemistry, but before she could convince herself to get the book out of her pack, Danny and Susan sat down a few feet from her.

Sighing, Kelly stood.

"We're not chasing you off, are we?" Danny asked.

"Of course not," Kelly said. "I need to stretch my legs, but I'll be back. Don't let my leaving interfere with anything." She left her books and wandered off. It could be Danny, she thought. But he doesn't look all that upset about us breaking up. He sure found someone else in a hurry.

She walked around campus for a while, thinking unproductively. Eventually she noticed Tad sitting alone, watching the outdoor half of the Phys Ed finals. She hesitated.

I do have a date with him, she reminded herself. It wouldn't hurt to say hi. And I'm probably being unfair, anyway. He asks a few innocent questions and I start thinking he's playing games.

"Hi," she told him. "You're looking thoughtful."

"Listen," he said.

Kelly listened. From far off she could hear faint popping noises. "Sounds almost like gunshots," she said.

"Firecrackers. Jeff and some of his friends celebrating early. There's another group running around shaking up cans of soda pop and squirting people."

"Just think," Kelly said. "Those are the next senators, governors, and corporate leaders. Our nation can be proud."

Tad grinned and Kelly found herself smiling in response. He patted the ground next to him and Kelly sat. "I'm almost afraid to have them at my house tomorrow," he said. "Imagine what they'll be like when this is all over. We've all been so tense this week."

"Compressed," Kelly agreed.

"That's it! Compressed. By tomorrow night we'll have sealed our fates, good or bad, and there won't be any more questions. We'll know whether we've made it or not. Even if we don't make it, just the fact that nothing's on the line anymore will be enough to release the pressure."

"Don't tell me you're worried about making it," Kelly said. "You're number one in the whole class!"

"I'm only number one as long as I keep making the best grades," Tad pointed out. "There's always someone behind me, waiting for me to goof up. And the second I do, I'm not first anymore. And besides, I'm only number one here, in this school, in this class, this year. There are thousands of number ones, Kelly. One at each high school in the country, every year. Year after year."

"It still seems pretty impressive to me," Kelly said.

Tad glanced sideways at her. "Not really," he said. "I've been thinking about grades. Who's been thinking about anything else this week? You know what I realized? Grades are only one measure. Like a yardstick. If you used a meterstick, you'd get a different result. Grades measure how well we take tests. That's all. So being number one in the class means I'm number one at giving the expected answer."

Kelly made a face. "And that's impressive," she said. "I'm so bad at handling pressure that even when I know the expected answer I can't write it down."

"But you said it helped to pretend like you were taking the test for someone else. Right?"

Kelly nodded. "It helped."

"So what had changed? It was still a test. The same test, even. The pressure was still there. The only thing that changed was how you saw the pressure. Your perception of it."

Kelly looked at him, startled.

"It's true, isn't it?"

She nodded slowly. "I guess so."

"Where's your hat?" Tad asked. "I kept thinking you looked different, but I couldn't figure out why. It's the hat."

Kelly ran her hand over her head. "I must have left it with my books," she said. "I'd better go, anyway. It's almost time for my last class. Time to go see if I can convince my perceptions that the pressure isn't on me to take my Chem final."

"Good luck."

"Is that all it is? Luck?" Kelly asked.

The first bell rang as she got back to her books.

My hat isn't here! Kelly thought as she snagged up her pack.

Danny and Susan were gone, too, heading back to the building. Maybe they know what happened to it, Kelly thought, breaking into a run.

22

"Hey, Suze, wait up," Kelly called.

Susan paused, grabbing Danny's arm to stop him, too.

"My hat," Kelly said. "It was with my books. Did you see it? It's gone."

Susan frowned. "I don't remember it," she said.

"Did you see anyone there? Was anyone looking at my stuff?"

"We didn't stay," Susan said. "We . . . took a walk after you left. Are you sure about your hat? Maybe you left it somewhere else."

"I left it there," Kelly said.

"I don't remember seeing it," Susan said. "Did you, Danny?"

Danny shook his head.

"I've got a final to take," Kelly said. "Darn it. But I need to look for my hat. Maybe the wind came up and blew it somewhere. I'd better look." She shook her head, her eyes closed. "I can't go look. I have to take my final."

Her mind was almost a blank, but Kelly knew

she had to get to class and take her test. She ran for the building, sliding into her seat seconds before the bell rang.

The instructions were on the board, the same ones the teacher had told the class on Wednesday, repeated on Thursday. "Get your books ready. No talking. No questions. Do not leave your seat or your test is automatically over. I've said all I have to say. It's your turn to show how well you've listened. Good luck."

Wordlessly the teacher handed out the exams.

Kelly looked at the test. I can do it, she thought, commanding the knots in her stomach to subside. I did it in English. I can do it in Chemistry. I can take a test. Refocus my perception, right? It's just a homework paper. For Talia. I'm just doing a work sheet.

She took a few deep breaths and read the first question.

I know where to find that information, she thought, relaxing a little. In the chapter with the table of elements. Chapter five? Six?

She picked up the Chemistry book and opened it to the middle. *Janet paused and looked over her shoulder*, Kelly read silently. *The pack was regrouping, staring in her direction.*

What? Kelly thought blankly.

She shook her head. I'm going crazy, she thought. She looked at the page again but it said the same thing.

I must be crazy.

She flipped to the front of the book. Page 27?

How can it start on . . . this is not my Chemistry book!

She turned the book over. The cover said, *Chemistry in the World Today*, but the inside pages were from a different book.

She stared at the book, her mind churning. *No talking. No questions. I've said all I have to say.*

Kelly felt suddenly empty, the only reality the twisted knots inside and the words on the pages of what was not her Chemistry text, even if it bore the cover.

She closed the book, put it neatly in her pack, stood, and walked out of the classroom.

23

She stood, scratching her head, staring at the Ford.

I knew it wasn't the clutch assembly, she thought. There wasn't enough wrong with it to cause the noise. Still, I guess I was hoping that replacing it would make *some* difference. It didn't.

And I know it isn't the transmission.

But it's something. I flunked my Chemistry final. The noise has to be coming from somewhere. I pulled the transmission and the car made the same noise. That eliminates the transmission! And with that gone it sounded even more like the pressure plate. But I replaced the pressure plate and it didn't help. Somebody sabotaged my book so I would flunk. It was deliberate.

She heard Susan emerge from the house, heard her footsteps as she crunched across the gravel beside Kelly's work slab.

"It's Tad this time," Susan said. "Talia called again, too."

"Take a message, will you?" Kelly asked.

"They don't want to leave messages," Susan said. "They want to talk to you."

"Would you please just tell them I'm fine, I'm busy, and I don't feel like talking?" Kelly repositioned the transmission jack. "I'm greasy. I'm under the car. I don't want company."

"I thought you already took the transmission out," Susan said.

Kelly looked at her, surprised. "I didn't know you kept track," she said. "I'm doing it again. I need something to do. I'm just going to check and make sure I did it right the first time."

"You did it right," Susan said. "You don't make mistakes. Daddy said so."

"Everybody makes mistakes," Kelly said, scooting the tray of tools closer to the car. "Even Dad does. I know I do." She flopped onto the creeper, worming herself under the Ford.

Susan crunched back across the gravel.

What was that all about? Kelly wondered. She didn't make any snide comments. She didn't even sound impatient, and that's not the Susan I know. Speaking of Susan, what about Danny? He takes Chemistry. He'd know which text I needed. He and Susan were both right there. One or both of them could have switched the book . . . and taken my hat.

She pulled the transmission again, took the clutch assembly apart, put everything back together. She didn't find anything wrong with the job she had done, or with the new clutch, but she hadn't expected to. Every so often the thoughts would creep into her mind — *I flunked my Chemistry final. Somebody wanted me to flunk my Chemistry final* — and she pushed them aside, wiping clutch pieces instead, tightening bolts.

Tomorrow's the end, she thought, cleaning her hands. She shivered. I hope not literally. But . . . it's the last chance for freak accidents and attacks. I'd better be on guard.

She made sure the chain was latched on the front door to the house, double-checked her bedroom window, and propped a chair beneath her bedroom doorknob before she went to bed.

Just in case, she thought.

Friday

24

Is it over? Did I win?

They were going to trap me, but I was too clever. She and the principal plotted, but I plotted better. And faster. Having everyone ask me how well I did . . . did they think I would confess? That was an easy trap! They didn't make very good traps. Saying I had a message in the office! How dumb do they think I am? Is that all they could think of? Waiting for me to trip up and confess or walk into the lair?

Two times she went to the office! But she only had dumb traps. Easy traps. And I was so worried!

My traps were so much better!

She'll flunk Chemistry and Spanish. She doesn't know about Spanish yet, but she'll find out. And if she was scared enough, she might have flunked the English test, too. She should have been scared enough. I got her good!

Then she can talk all she wants but nobody will believe her. She'll be a loser, and nobody believes in a loser.

I won't flunk English. I know they wanted me to have a perfect test so they could catch me. I wanted to have a perfect test, too, but I didn't. I did just exactly well enough to win and no more. I was too smart. That means I won. I did win!

I defeated the enemy and I am the winner!

25

Friday at lunch, Kelly took her tray outside and sat with Talia.

"Hi," she said.

"You're speaking to me?" Talia asked.

"Sorry about last night," Kelly said. "I wasn't feeling sociable."

"So Susan said."

Kelly explained about the Chemistry final.

"How bizarre!" Talia said. "Who could have done that, Kelly? What's going on?"

"I don't know," Kelly said, listening carefully to Talia's voice, watching her face. She's not involved, Kelly thought. She can't be. "It got worse," she added. "Worse than flunking the Chem final."

"How?"

"First tell me what time the party starts," Kelly said.

"Five-thirty," Talia said. "Hamburgers grilling from five-thirty to seven or so. Swimming anytime. Dancing after about seven o'clock."

"I may make it for dancing, then," Kelly said.

"How it gets worse is like this: Computer Lit. Conference with the teacher. 'Kelly, I printed out a hard copy of everyone's final so they could see why they got the grades they got. Yours was pretty interesting. Here. Why don't you take a look?' And she hands me instructions for pulling a transmission and removing and examining a clutch assembly."

"What? Why did she give you that?"

"It's what I typed," Kelly said, smiling grimly. "Instead of typing the pages she'd assigned, I'd typed what I was thinking about."

"I don't believe it!" Talia tried to keep her expression serious, but finally gave up, bursting into laughter. "Only you!" she gasped, holding her stomach. "Nobody else would have done it."

Reluctantly Kelly grinned. "Okay, it was a little bit amusing," she said. "Now I have to decide whether to take the test over or take a C. At least the teacher had a sense of humor. She said the computer computed my speed and accuracy at a B, but since I'd done the wrong assignment she'd have to lower my grade. So I can take the C or take the test over."

"It's pretty nice of her to give you a choice. What are you going to do? You had a high B in that class, didn't you? Are you going to settle for a C on your final?"

"I don't know," Kelly said. "A C may be the best I can do on a final. Compared to my other finals, a C is good. I got a D+ in Geometry, in spite of the fact that I know it a lot better than that. I had a B in Geometry before the final. I got a D+ on my History final, too. That was my A class. I'm not setting any records with my final grades, Tee."

"How about Spanish? What happened there? You sounded good when we studied. Why did you get called up for a conference in class? You looked pretty grim when you got done."

"I did fine on the oral portion," Kelly said. "But Talia, he didn't have my written test."

"What? Didn't you hand it in?"

She sure sounds innocent, Kelly thought, hating herself for her suspicions. "I was in the third lab group," she said. "I left my test facedown on my desk, like we were supposed to. When I got back, the tests had been collected. That's all I know. But mine never got turned in."

"I don't understand," Talia said. "That doesn't make sense. What happened to your test?"

Kelly shrugged. "It could have gotten shuffled in with something else. Could have fallen out of the folder. Or else someone took it. Stole it. That's all I can figure. Luckily, the teacher saw it. He was walking around looking at tests, and he remembers looking at mine."

"That's great! How lucky can you get?"

"I still have to take it over," Kelly said. "I'm glad I get to, but it's just another reason I may be very late tonight. I may be here forever, having conferences."

They stood as the bell rang, heading back into the school. "I'll see you tonight," Talia told Kelly. "Whenever you make it."

Kelly reached up to readjust her hat and let her hand fall, feeling foolish for the automatic gesture. No hat, she thought. No hat, no test.

The table was gone from her English classroom, the books that had been on it piled on the floor instead.

"Pass around yearbooks if you like," Mrs. Beckman said. "I'll be doing conferences. Kelly, I'd like to talk with you first, please."

Perplexed, Kelly took the seat near the teacher's desk. What now? she thought. I didn't sign up for a conference in here.

"I didn't think I did that bad," Kelly said.

"Badly," Mrs. Beckman said automatically. "No, you didn't. In fact, you had some rather interesting comments on your test. Unexpectedly interesting. You don't usually . . . um, shine on tests."

"I know," Kelly agreed. "Tests make me nervous."

"I know you didn't sign up for a conference," Mrs. Beckman said. "And I need to use class time for the people who did. But would you please stop by after school?"

"I have another after-school commitment," Kelly said.

"It's important. I'm afraid I can't give you a final grade until after we've discussed a few things."

"I don't understand," Kelly said.

"Please stop by after school. After your other commitment. I'll be here."

"Okay," Kelly said, frowning. What does she want? What's gone wrong now?

26

The last day of school, Kelly thought. It's nothing but one long conference session and yearbook-signing party. Nobody seems to care about attendance as long as we turn in our books and get the checkout forms signed.

Seniors wandered the halls or lounged outside on the grass and benches. Kelly was scheduled for timed tests in Phys Ed, so she headed for the locker room to change, waving at friends who were wandering the campus with no place to be, no conferences, nothing to do but talk or watch the timed tests.

The last day is a waste, Kelly thought, reporting to the track. No one does anything. We cry about our grades and check in our books. Big deal. There really wasn't any point in showing up today. Of course, if yesterday had been the last day, it would have been the same waste. I guess there has to be a wasted last day, and this is it.

Suddenly she realized that no odd accidents had happened all day. There had been no vandalism, no collapsing tables, no hidden threats.

That's too weird, she thought. It's the last day. Whoever it is doing these things should have done something today. Why didn't they? They can't have just given up as suddenly as they started. Can they?

Phys Ed is a good time to play tricks on someone, she thought, nervously eyeing the crowded field. It's easy to trip someone while they're running, or booby-trap the field so someone falls. There are so many people wandering around. Nobody would remember one person. Nobody would know if someone didn't belong here.

She edged herself into the second group for the 600-meter walk/run so she'd have time while the first group was running to look for anything odd on the track. She did the same thing for the various dashes, hurdles, and jumps, alert for anything suspicious.

They moved indoors for the skill and flexibility tests, and Kelly looked around, still nervous, still convinced that something would go wrong. She dribbled the basketball, shooting from various stations around the gym, watching for traps, hoping she'd recognize them before she got caught in them. She sat behind the tape and let her partner measure her reach as she leaned forward, wondering when the attack would occur, if she could sidestep in time.

Why hasn't anything happened? she thought as they formed groups for the marathon-endurance-aerobic-skills tests, as the teacher called the last section. The groups would spend ninety seconds at each of eight stations, running for the next station each time the whistle blew.

Kelly's group started at the chairs where they were supposed to step up onto the chair seat, then back down, rapidly, alternating the leading leg with each set. Kelly grabbed the chair and shook it before she put her weight on it. It seemed sturdy. When she stepped on it, it held her.

They couldn't have known which chair I'd be using, she told herself. Whoever it is, they're after *me*, not just anyone.

She ran for the jump ropes at the whistle, thinking, There's no way to booby-trap jump ropes. Tampering with the gym equipment may be a good way to hurt someone, but it's too random. They don't know which piece of equipment I'll use.

She told herself the same thing through the aerobics-with-weights station, then the running relays across the gym.

Everybody's been using the exercise bikes, she thought, reaching automatically to tighten the seat knob. It was loose, but the knobs were always loose after the bikes had been used.

Her cheeks felt flushed, her breathing had settled into a familiar rhythm, her muscles responding smoothly to each command. She hopped from the bike to run to the calisthenics station, doing the old-fashioned jumping jacks and waist pivots, the side stretches, and shoulder rolls, thinking, I'm safe. No one is going to hurt me here. I'm going to be fine.

At the whistle she headed for the stairs, looking

carefully to be sure nothing was spilled on them, that there were no pieces of paper or spots of oil to slip on.

You're being paranoid, she told herself. You're safe. You're in a crowd of friends. No one will hurt you here.

She held her hand so it skimmed the railing anyway, just in case she needed to grab something suddenly, just in case someone tried to trip or push her down. Her legs were beginning to protest but she ignored them except to be sure they lifted high enough that she didn't trip herself.

The whistle blew again, and she ran to the ropes, thick, knotted lines that hung from the ceiling, lines still swinging from the last group.

Kelly grabbed a rope and leaped up, wrapping her legs around the line, pulling herself up hand over hand, using her legs both to propel herself upward and to keep from sliding backward.

The last station of the last test of the last day of Phys Ed, she thought. *What if the rope breaks?*

The thought jolted her out of her concentrated effort, and she faltered.

It can't break, she told herself. It's too thick.

What if it unravels?

She glanced up at the ceiling, forcing herself to keep her hands moving, each time grasping a hold farther up. As far up as she could see, the rope looked whole and sound.

There are no weak spots. The rope is fine. But someone is after me and they could get me easily while I'm hanging here. They could be up there with a file, sawing at the rope, making it fray. *Don't be stupid. There's no one up there.*

What if it comes untied at the top? Who checks that knot, way up there? What if the knot is loose? Would I even feel it coming undone? Hand up. Let go. Grab again. Rewrap legs. *Just do it, Kelly. Climb.*

The pounding of feet from people at other stations, the noise — the shouting of spectators, the squeals, squeaks and rattles, hums and clangs of equipment — seemed to focus itself in the rope, in a line that suddenly seemed too fragile and thin to support Kelly's weight as she dangled far above the gymnasium floor.

I'm afraid, Kelly acknowledged to herself, closing her eyes. *Someone is trying to hurt me and I'm afraid. I'm afraid to fall. I don't want to get any higher up. The higher up I am, the farther I can fall.*

The rope thrummed in her hands, vibrating.

Climb, she told herself. She grabbed the rope higher up, rewrapped her legs, pulled.

If I fall, I'll be a broken, bloody mess.

Hand up. Pull.

The whistle blew, signaling the end of time, the end of the test.

Hand up. Pull. *I'm going to the top.*

"Kelly. It's over. Come on down."

It's not over, Kelly thought, finally opening her eyes. *It isn't over at all. Hand over hand. Pull.*

"Kelly!"

Kelly ignored her classmates, slowly gathering

her fear and focusing it into determination, using all her determination to continue up, hand over hand.

I'm going to the top. If I fall, I'll fall from the top.

27

And then she was there. At the top. There was no one there with a file, fraying the rope. The knot was not only firm, it was double-tied, rewoven back into itself, and crimped with thick metal staples.

Reassured and satisfied, Kelly began her descent, reversing the hand over hand, sliding even though the rope scraped her thighs and burned her hands.

"You kind of froze halfway up," the teacher commented.

"Yeah," Kelly agreed, feeling embarrassed and relieved at the same time. I'm safe, she thought. No one hurt me.

The teacher nodded, her eyes expressing what she didn't put into words. *You were afraid, but you did it anyway.*

"Here's your pass," she said, handing Kelly the slip of pink paper. "You'll be late after you shower and check out."

Kelly took the slip, smiling, feeling a warm satisfaction.

"In case you're curious, you got an A on your final," the gym teacher told her. "Even if you did take longer than ninety seconds on that last station."

Kelly signed out of Phys Ed and headed for her last class, almost dazzled by the thought of an A on a final exam. But the excitement faded as she entered the Chemistry classroom. I sure didn't get an A in here, she thought, taking her seat. I flunked my final in here. And to top it off, I'll probably have to pay for my book since it's ruined. It was checked out to me. I'll have to pay for it.

She rummaged in her book bag, but didn't feel any books in it at all. She hauled it up on her desk and looked, pushing aside the paraphernalia from the school year.

I put the book in here, she thought. I didn't touch it. I haven't touched it since yesterday. Where is it?

Finally she dumped the pack on her desk, stuffing things back into the pack one by one. The Chemistry book was not there.

This is ridiculous! she thought. What if I was so tense and worried that I hallucinated the whole thing? But I didn't. I know I didn't. Someone deliberately took my book, cut it apart, and glued another book inside. And then they stole it back so I wouldn't have any proof! Someone made me flunk my final and then made sure no one would believe me if I told.

She sighed, feeling incredibly stupid. And I played right into their hands, she thought, leaving my bag lying around at lunch all day where anyone could get at it, even while I was being so suspicious and worrying that they were thinking up a trick.

Suddenly she was angry. They tried to make sure I couldn't tell, she thought. Well, I'm telling anyway, proof or no proof. She stood and marched to the teacher's desk. "I'd like a conference," she announced.

The teacher looked up at her. "I was hoping you would," she said. "I'm not too tightly scheduled. I can fit you in during class. Add your name to the list."

When her turn for a conference came Kelly said, "The reason I walked out yesterday was because someone deliberately sabotaged my Chemistry book."

She went on, reminding the teacher about the no talking, no questions rules.

"Am I so inflexible that you didn't think an extraordinary circumstance merited an exception? A sabotaged book should have been mentioned, Kelly, no matter what I'd said."

"You were very firm about the instructions," Kelly said. "You even put them on the board. Anyway, it doesn't matter now. I know I flunked the test, and I know I'll have to pay for the book. And it makes me mad that someone made me flunk and then stole the book back so I don't have any proof. It makes me mad that they're going to get away with it."

"That's a pretty serious charge, deliberately causing someone to flunk."

Kelly smiled grimly. "I'm not charging anyone in particular," she said. "Because I have no idea who did it. It's almost too fantastic to believe. Even I have trouble believing it and I saw it."

The bell rang and noise erupted from the halls. Seniors cheered and shouted, celebrating the last bell of the last day.

"Well," Kelly said. "Here's the money for the book. And here's my checkout slip. Will you keep an eye on it, please? That piece of paper is my ticket out of here and I don't want it mysteriously disappearing, too."

A sudden thought took unpleasant form. "How much was the final worth?" Kelly asked. "You said thirty percent of the grade, right? And I had a B in here."

"You didn't just flunk the final, Kelly. You got a zero."

Kelly slumped in her chair, shaking her head. Out in the halls the seniors' voices rose in triumph as they screamed and cheered, ripping and tossing papers and notebooks, chanting happily.

"The zero brought your B to an F."

All the warmth Kelly had felt at her A in Phys Ed evaporated, leaving a chill even in the heat of the late May afternoon.

"You don't need this class to graduate," the teacher said. "It's an elective, Kelly. A lot of colleges require Chemistry, but it isn't essential. But, under the circumstances, I think we can make some arrangements if you want the credit . . . but it'll mean coming back to school next week."

"You'd let me take the test over?" Kelly asked. "Even after I walked out? Even after you've given all the tests back?"

"I'd let you take it over again right now, except that I don't have time. But we can work something out. Come in Monday. We'll do something."

Kelly made her way through her exuberant classmates, answering their shouts and smiles as best she could, wishing she were going home, too, instead of to another conference. She headed for the stairs, for the Spanish room, for more bad news about another sabotaged final. Congratulations? she thought. You guys may be done here, but I guess I'm not. I thought all I had to do was make it through this week, but that didn't turn out to be enough.

"I never saw such childish behavior." It was Talia's voice, angry and intense.

Kelly couldn't see Talia. The comment had come from a doorway in the hall ahead of her and Kelly couldn't see who her friend was talking to. She paused, not wanting to interrupt, not sure whether she should walk by without saying hello.

"I've had just about enough and I'm going to tell Kelly so," Talia said.

A wave of weakness dropped over Kelly, a sad, disappointed feeling that made her turn away to avoid hearing any more.

"It's her father's hat. Since he's never around, it's important to Kelly to have something. I guess if my father weren't around . . ."

That's Jeffrey, Kelly thought, hurrying back down the hall to get away from the conversation. Is he defending me? Or making fun?

"She was almost hysterical, and what was the point . . ."

Shut up, Talia, Kelly thought, biting her lip. Just shut up. She plunged through a crowd of seniors, trying to smile and return their happy greetings.

So that's what Talia's been trying to tell me, she thought. Everything's ending, she said. I didn't realize she meant our friendship, too. How stupid can I get? I didn't even see the warning signs.

28

She pushed open the door to the Spanish classroom and sat in the desk nearest the teacher's.

He didn't smile. "What do you think happened to your final?" he asked.

"I think someone deliberately stole it so I'd flunk," Kelly said.

"In twenty years of teaching I have never lost a test or homework paper," he said. "Though I've had students try to convince me I did. So, even though it is a nasty, spiteful thing to steal someone's test, I agree, that's what happened. The question is, who did such a thing?"

Talia's in my Spanish class, Kelly thought. She hated the idea but once it had lodged in her thoughts, it stayed there.

"Jealousy is not an uncommon reason for such an act," the teacher said. "But you are not in competition for a number one rating. Do you suppose it could have been random? Someone who wanted to do a mean thing grabbed a test and it was only incidental that it belonged to you?"

Random? Kelly thought, shaking her head. No. This is not random. "I wish I could believe that," she said sadly. "But I don't."

"Nor do I. You will have to take the test again, Kelly. You understand that?"

"Yes. I'm glad you're going to let me, even if it does mean I have to take it twice."

The teacher looked at her thoughtfully. "It is not good to be the victim of a . . . prank. If you can come Monday, you can take the test over. I'm sorry that it's necessary."

"You had some interesting things to say on your final," Mrs. Beckman said.

Kelly looked at her English teacher, waiting. What's her point? she wondered. Why did she say I wouldn't get a grade unless I came in?

Mrs. Beckman didn't go on, so finally Kelly said, "Good interesting or bad interesting? I thought I did pretty well on the final."

"You did. I was surprised."

"Me, too, actually," Kelly admitted, thinking of the collapsing table.

"Why do you suppose you did so well?"

Kelly frowned. "Is there a problem?" she asked. "Was my test okay?"

"It was more than okay," Mrs. Beckman said. "And that's surprising, Kelly. You don't usually do well on tests. And to have you suddenly hand in a well-thought-out, comprehensive, and original exam when you usually give scanty, sketchy answers is . . . well, it's odd."

"I see," Kelly said. "It's odd for me to do well, so because I did, it's somehow suspicious?"

"That's putting it bluntly. But yes."

"I don't understand what you're telling me," Kelly said. "Or asking me. I'm glad I did well! Tests scare me. To do well on a final is a major accomplishment. Especially on an English final!"

"Maybe you could kind of let me in on your thought processes," Mrs. Beckman said. "If I could understand how you came to give superior answers, it would help me clarify things in my own mind."

Kelly frowned. This is certainly strange, she thought. But what else could I expect? Life has been strange! She thought back to the day of the final. "Someone took the screws out of the table so it would collapse when I sat on it."

Mrs. Beckman looked startled.

"That scared me," Kelly said, musing aloud. "I'd been trying to figure out why someone was playing pranks on me and whether they were personal attacks. Something pretty serious had happened the night before and I was getting suspicious about everything. I was watching everyone, wondering if they secretly hated me. So that question about the antagonist representing the hero's dark side made me start wondering about the dark things people carry around with them."

She frowned again. "It didn't make sense that things should start happening for no reason at all, so somehow I must have hurt someone, and now they're getting back at me."

Kelly looked at her English teacher and continued. "You know, we're not like the characters in the stories. Our problems aren't great and important like in literature, and the choices the characters make seem unreal to us. I mean, a golden fleece and a homemade monster? It's not real. The stories didn't mean much to me when I read them. But here I am, with a mysterious, secret enemy, and all of sudden the characters and the stories are more relevant. Everyone has a dark side they don't like looking at. And we're all antagonists."

Kelly shivered. I've certainly antagonized someone! she thought. "I'm not good at people," she said, still frowning. "I'm good at machines. Like cars. They're straightforward and simple. When they toss me a puzzle, I know I'm working with limited possibilities. A noise in the engine isn't going to be caused by the tires. And it's not going to be caused by hurt feelings or greed or any motive at all. I've got real things I can fix and replace and then I'm done. People aren't like that. They're . . . devious. They hide their feelings. They can have all kinds of things wrong with them and not make any noise at all. Give me a nice, clean, broken-down car any day!"

"Cars aren't very clean," Mrs. Beckman joked lightly. "And they seem pretty dark and mysterious to me."

"I'll take the cars, then," Kelly said. "You take the people."

"I'm sorry, Kelly," Mrs. Beckman said.

"For what?"

"I didn't realize you couldn't relate to the literature I chose. And I thought you might have cheated."

"How can you cheat on an essay test?" Kelly asked. "You can't. You'd have to wait for someone else to answer the questions, then try to read their answer, and then try to put it in your own words. It would be too hard and it would take too long."

"There's another way to cheat."

"How?" Kelly asked.

"Steal a copy of the final exam. Then you know the questions ahead of time and you have lots of time to look up answers and develop a line of reasoning."

"Oh," Kelly said. "But wouldn't you know if a copy of the test disappeared?"

"Yes," Mrs. Beckman said. "I did know. I missed it right away."

Kelly stared, eyes widening. "You mean someone did steal a copy? And you thought I did it?"

"I was very upset about it. I tried to figure out who had done it and it was driving me crazy. I finally realized all I had to do was wait for someone to do unexpectedly well on the final. You're the only one who did, Kelly. Some people did better than I'd figured they would, and some did worse, but no one had the sudden, unexpected insights that you had. You really surprised me."

"Oh," Kelly said. "Now I see what you were getting at. I don't like tests. I especially don't like final tests. And of all the final tests I don't like, I don't like English the most! But I did not cheat. As much as I hated flunking last year's final, I'd flunk again before I'd cheat."

"I believe you," Mrs. Beckman said. "You were a good suspect. You were in the right place at the right time to have stolen the final, and you did better than expected on the test. But I believe you. And that's rather unfortunate, because now my choices are to forget it, which I cannot do, or to question everyone who did even a little bit better on the final than expected. And that will be quite an undertaking since the seniors have been released from school already."

Kelly sighed as she left the classroom. This is the most bizarre day of my whole life, she thought. I wish it were already over and I was home in bed, asleep.

29

Is it over? Is it over? I can't tell if it's over. Didn't I win? I thought I won. Didn't I? Did I?

30

Kelly stopped by her locker for the final time. Even though the administration had made the usual announcements forbidding it, the seniors had still strewn the hall with papers and notebooks, littering it ankle deep.

The locker doors up and down the hall hung open, gaping like rows of empty coffins, their lids ajar.

The senior class exists no more, Kelly thought, gathering the few papers and odds and ends left on her locker shelves. She pried the mirror off the door and dropped it into her book bag, started stripping the posters and signs from the locker walls. She looked at the poster that had been sprayed with squirt-cheese. She'd wiped it, but there was still a yellow smudge.

"There's no hope for it," she muttered, crumpling it.

"There's always hope," Danny said from behind her.

Kelly jumped, whacking her arm on the locker door.

"Sorry," Danny said. "Didn't mean to scare you."

"What are you doing here?" Kelly asked. "Everyone's gone home."

"I was looking for you," he admitted. "I want to talk to you." He put his hands on her shoulders. "About us," he added.

Kelly was horrified to feel her stomach tighten at his touch. Her breath felt ragged in her throat. " 'Us' doesn't mean anything anymore," she managed to tell him.

"But I want it to," Danny said. "I've missed you, Kel."

Kelly fought the impulse to throw her arms around him and never let go. *Danny,* she thought. *It would feel so good to have someone hold me right about now.*

As if sensing her thoughts Danny bent down and kissed her, tentatively at first, as if he wasn't sure how she'd react.

It feels so natural, Kelly thought.

Danny's arms tightened around her.

Suddenly Kelly felt smothered. She had a vivid image of Danny and Susan kissing in the car, remembered Tad's understanding comment.

Confused, she broke away from Danny.

"What's wrong?" he asked, reaching for her again.

She stepped back, almost leaning into her still-open locker. "Don't," she said.

"Why not? You liked it. I could tell."

"Maybe I did. But that's my problem, and I can handle it."

"What's to handle?" Danny asked. "We're getting back together where we belong. There's no problem."

"Yes, there is," Kelly said. "We're not getting back together, Danny. It's over, and it's going to stay over."

Danny's face darkened. "You still care about me," he insisted. "I could tell. I know you, Kelly. I know you better than anyone else does."

He's right, she thought. I guess I do still care, whether I want to or not. And I don't want to.

"You want me," Danny said.

Kelly shrugged. She turned and stripped another sign from her locker wall, unable to concentrate long enough to read it.

"Let's go somewhere together," Danny urged. "We can finish talking this over. We need to talk."

"I already have a date," she said.

"With Tad? If we're getting back together you'll have to drop him, you know. Just tell him you're going somewhere with me tonight. We'll skip the party. It'll be just you and me."

"We're not getting back together," Kelly said.

"Taking any bets?" Danny asked tersely. "I want you back, Kelly. And I get what I want."

"No, you don't," Kelly told him. "You take it. And you can't just take me, Danny. I'm not up for grabs." She shut her locker firmly.

Danny's fists clenched. He slammed one against the metal door, adding another dent to the gray surface.

Kelly gave him a level, angry stare. "You can't

solve problems with fists," she said. "Maybe you'll learn that some day." He's a senior, she thought. Why does he act like a five-year-old? Tad wouldn't have done that.

The thought gave her the determination she needed to walk away from Danny, and she walked quickly, afraid if she waited . . . if he kissed her again, she might not leave at all.

What's the matter with me? she thought, disgusted. How can I be so sure I don't want him and still react like that? Doesn't my opinion count? I don't want him back!

"Hi," Susan said when Kelly walked into the house. "You're going to be late to the party." She made a face. "So am I, I guess. Have you seen Danny?"

Kelly felt a stab of guilt. Yeah, she thought. I saw him. I let him kiss me. He asked me to go out with him. He was willing to leave you waiting here alone while he took your sister out somewhere to talk her into getting back together with him. "I left school about four-thirty," she told Susan, bending down to scratch behind Grease's ears. "I saw him then, in the halls. I don't know if he was leaving or not."

The phone rang, and Susan jumped to answer it. "Oh, hi," she said, and Kelly knew it wasn't Danny.

"No, I'm not disappointed it's you. Yes, she's here. Love you, too." Susan handed the phone to Kelly, her eyes glistening with tears. When Kelly took the phone, Susan ran upstairs.

"Hi, Dad," Kelly said. "Yeah, I've been thinking about it. . . . Dad, exactly what would they let me do?"

She listened for a minute, frowning in thought, her cat winding itself around her legs. "I don't know," she said. "That's pretty basic stuff. . . . I understand, Dad. I don't expect big jobs the first summer." But I'd have big jobs if I worked here, for myself, she thought.

"When do you have to have an answer?" she asked. "Okay. Call me back tomorrow. I'll tell you then. . . . I love you, too. 'Bye."

"Are you going to take the job?" Susan called, her voice coming from the stairs.

"Don't know," Kelly answered. "I think Danny's here, Suze. I hear his car."

"Will you get the door?" Susan asked, her voice coming from the direction of the bathroom.

Kelly nodded, though she knew Susan couldn't see her. Of course I'll get the door, she thought. Why shouldn't I add one more disaster to today? Why shouldn't I just open the door for Danny and say hi again? Why was Susan being so polite? She wasn't even nasty-polite, just plain-old-ordinary-regular-polite. What's going on?

I don't want to know, she reminded herself. No people puzzles, remember?

Danny rang the bell and Kelly opened the door. Grease rocketed by her, escaping the confines of the house.

"Oh, no!" Kelly yelped, pushing past Danny. "She's not supposed to be outside!"

31

Kelly scanned the yard.

"There!" Danny pointed. Grease was rolling in the dirt by the corner of the house.

"Don't chase her," Kelly warned. "She'll run." She nodded to her left. "Circle that way." She headed right, in an arc, not even looking at the cat.

She and Danny were both about five feet from Grease, closing in on her, when the cat streaked between them and disappeared under the disabled Ford.

Kelly started after her. I don't feel like playing tag, she thought, disgusted with herself for not paying attention when she opened the door.

She shaded her eyes from the sun, trying to peer under the car. The cat made a motionless, shadowy lump behind the rear tire. Kelly lunged and caught the lump, but it was not a furry, breathing cat.

Kelly pulled the familiar shape out into the sunlight, staring without comprehension at her hat.

"I got her," Danny said, coming up behind Kelly.

"She scratched me good . . . what's that? Oh, Kelly! What happened?"

As Kelly looked at her hat the slashes came into focus, each ruined shred of the crown etching itself in her mind as if burned there.

She dropped the hat and backed away from it, her eyes wide, her breath caught in her throat as if it had forgotten how to flow in and out of her lungs. No! she thought. Not this. Not slashes. These are knife cuts.

"Kelly! Snap out of it!" Danny ordered.

The air in her lungs escaped in a sob. Danny handed her the cat and then wrapped his arms around her, holding her, patting her back and shoulders. Kelly cradled Grease as if the black fur were the ruined hat, stroking it gently.

"You okay now?" Danny asked when Kelly stirred.

She nodded.

"What . . . ?" came Susan's voice.

Kelly hadn't heard her footsteps on the gravel. Oh, great, she thought tiredly, looking at her sister's hurt expression. Another misunderstanding to deal with. Danny couldn't have . . . no. It would have been too elaborate a plan to hide the hat hoping he'd be here when I found it so he could comfort me. It isn't Danny.

Susan glanced from Kelly to the hat, then back again, the hurt fading as indignation replaced it. "How rotten!" Susan said, snatching up the hat. "Who did this to Daddy's hat? Danny, help her inside."

134

Kelly was too astonished to protest as Danny stood and swung her up in his arms, carrying both her and the cat into the house. He plunked her on the couch, grinning. His grin faded as Susan entered the room.

"I could have walked," Kelly said.

"You looked like you were going to faint," Susan said.

"It's true," Danny added, his grin widening again.

"I've never fainted in my life," Kelly protested.

"I'm sorry about your hat," Susan said. "I'm sorry about a lot of things."

Susan looked like she was going to say something else, then instead, smiled broadly — the wide, social smile Kelly found more irritating than a door slammed in her face.

"I'm ready to go now, Danny," Susan said. "If we're still going."

"Are you okay now?" Danny asked Kelly.

She nodded. "Go ahead," she said. "If you see Tad, tell him I'll be along later, okay? Oh . . . I'd appreciate it if you didn't mention the hat. I don't want to talk about it. And if everybody knows, they'll all be asking me questions."

"Sure," Danny said.

Susan's fake smile widened. "Sure," she echoed.

After they left Kelly wandered back out to the Ford. When was I supposed to find it? she wondered. Since we're all going to Tad's tonight, was I supposed to find it before the party or later? Tomorrow? Does it matter?

She looked longingly at Mrs. Rider's car. I could just crawl under it and start taking things apart, she thought. I'm not exactly in a party mood, but I can always play with a car.

She lifted the hood. That noise is a metallic grating or a metallic rattle. The noise is definitely coming from the transmission area, but it is definitely *not* anything in that area. It has to be something else. But what? Something else. Something somewhere else. Almost as devious as a person, huh? Masking the problem.

She pushed the thoughts aside. I'd have sworn it was the pressure plate, she thought, checking the bolts holding the fan to the water pump.

They're tight. I'm going to take the fan belt off. That'll at least eliminate a lot of potential sources of noise. Power steering and smog pumps and stuff. Maybe I can get a better idea what's happening if I cut out some of the other noises.

She loosened the alternator and pulled the fan belt off, then started the Ford.

"I'll be darned," she muttered, listening to the almost-silent car. "No noise. No funny noise at all!" Incredible! she thought, grinning. She shut the car off and grabbed two fan blades, wiggling them, yanking them up and down.

"The water pump!" she said, shaking her head. "The darned water pump! Why wasn't the little bugger leaking? How sneaky! That was a water pump noise, all right, except it was about ninety times too loud."

She laughed out loud at the car. "Thought you could fool me, huh?" she asked.

The day's problems had evaporated with her successful diagnosis. She tossed the fan belt onto the engine, closed the hood, and headed into the garage to clean her hands.

I don't know how, she thought, but the noise carried clear back to the transmission. It was vibrating there for some reason. How funny! It sure had me fooled! At least for a while there.

She locked the garage and went in the house to get her swimsuit and towel. I wonder what the percentage is of water pumps that go bad and don't leak? she thought, grabbing her windbreaker. She locked the house and tossed her things into the Thunderbird along with her purse.

It would have leaked in a few more days, she decided. If Mrs. Rider had kept driving it, it would have leaked. Then it would have been obvious.

She laughed again as she pulled her car away from the curb. I love it! she thought. Fooled by a water pump. I'll call Mrs. Rider in the morning and tell her she can have her car back tomorrow afternoon. What a good joke on me! A nonleaking water pump that sounded like a pressure plate.

She remembered her hat and sobered again.

I only solved one small problem, she told herself. The fun one. Now I have to figure out the rest of the problems. Like, who hates me enough to be doing these things to me.

32

Can it be over if she still has Winners?

She won't give up as long as she has it because now she knows that a winner never quits. She isn't finished with me.

It was weakness that made me think it was over. I hoped it was over. I'm forgetting everything I learned. They're still planning a trap. I can feel it. I can feel the bars coming down over me. How can I escape? Where will they trap me?

I know!

At the ceremonies! She won't graduate, but she can still go. She will go. She's planning a public trap! Just when I think I've won and that it's all over, they'll spring. They'll attack then, when I'm most vulnerable.

A winner thinks ahead to the finish line and sets the path firmly in mind. A winner does not weaken or stray until the battle is over. She will never give up as long as she lives.

I am the winner. I am the winner. I am the winner. I will do what must be done and I will win.

33

By the time Kelly arrived the party was in full forward gear. The pool, in the walk-out basement of the Sedalia's lavish house, was teeming with bodies and beach balls, the shouts, laughter, and splashing echoing off the walls.

Sliding glass doors opened to a sunken sun patio, with towel-wrapped people coming in and going out in a steady stream, heading toward the pool, the sauna, and the whirlpool. Some held plates of food and claimed benches or spots on the floor to sit and eat.

Kelly saw Jeff and Talia waving from the pool and waved back, still stinging from the bit of conversation she'd overheard. Susan and Danny emerged from the direction of the changing rooms, holding hands and smiling at each other. Music from an unseen sound system added to the party noise and the smell of chlorine mixed with the scent of grilling hamburgers pulled at Kelly, tugging her in different directions.

Should I eat or swim? she thought. That food smells good.

Tad pulled himself from the pool and splashed over to her. "Hi," he said, dripping noisily. "Come on in. It's great!"

"I think I'll change first," Kelly said.

"That's not really necessary," Tad told her. "I like you just the way you are." He grinned, reaching for her, but Kelly jumped backward.

"It's no trouble to change," she said. "Honest."

"Hurry, then."

Kelly stopped to say hello to friends as she made her way to the womens' shower and changing room. A few people were changing back into their street clothes, hanging damp towels on pegs. Kelly slipped on her suit and showered quickly, exchanging congratulations.

For nothing, she thought, reminded of the final exams she still had to take. It's not over for me.

She tried to shake off the sudden feeling that it would never be over, that she'd go on and on, taking finals over and over forever, with something happening each time so she had to do it again.

It can't happen, she told herself, grabbing her towel. I won't let it happen. I'm going to figure out who's behind all this and I'm going to stop them. Somehow.

She joined Tad in the pool and he promptly dunked her. She came up sputtering and chased him, intent on repayment. Talia called to her, but Kelly just waved again, feeling saddened.

She turned her attention back to Tad, finally

managing to dunk him, leaping backward to escape, bumping into Danny.

"How about a midnight swim?" someone shouted, and all the lights went out.

There were a few giggles and some laughter and then Kelly felt a sudden blow in the middle of her back. She tried to call out. She took a deep breath to yell, but all that came out were bubbles and a desperate gurgle.

This is all wrong, she told herself. Why am I under the water?

She tried to get up to the life-sustaining air, but there was a weight on her back and shoulders. She thrashed, but it didn't help. She tried to flip over but the weight was heavy . . . purposeful.

The incredible truth sank into her waterlogged awareness. But it was a vague thought, not urgent. As she slipped closer to unconsciousness it didn't seem terribly important.

Someone's trying to drown me.

34

Her lungs heaved, demanding air. She had just enough sense left to realize she mustn't breathe while she was underwater.

And then suddenly she was gasping and coughing, gulping precious oxygen. The lights were back on, the weight was gone from her back. Near her she could hear more choking and coughing.

"What happened?" she croaked.

"I don't know," Talia answered, taking deep breaths. "I was coming to find you when the lights went out. I reached for Jeff. I think I smacked somebody. And then I slipped. I swallowed a bunch of water and I'm not sure what happened after that."

"Same here," Susan said. "I reached out for Danny. I don't know if I got him or someone else, but I grabbed somebody, then somebody grabbed me, and then I sank."

"It wasn't very funny, turning the lights out," Tad said. His face was angry. "I hope this doesn't mean people are getting out of control."

Kelly looked at the group around her — Tad,

Talia, Jeffrey, Susan, and Danny. Am I crazy? she wondered. These people are friends. They couldn't have tried to drown me!

As her fear faded Kelly decided it had to have been an accident. People were slipping and grabbing and trying to hold on, she reminded herself. I just happened to be in the middle of the pile. On the bottom!

"You okay, Kelly?" Tad asked, looking worried.

"Yeah, I guess I am," she said. "But I'm done swimming."

"Me, too. I'm hungry. Meet you at the grills?"

What really happened? Kelly asked herself, heading for the changing room again. I'd be stupid to decide it was just an accident — after the fire and the hat and the table collapsing — just because I don't want it to be any of my friends. My friends? How well do I know any of them?

I have to be logical about this.

She used the shampoo that was in the shower, washing the chlorine from her hair.

Tad, Talia, Jeffrey, Susan, and Danny. They were the only people near me in the pool. If someone tried to drown me, it had to be one of those people. Those same people are all in my Spanish class. Tad, Talia, Jeffrey, Susan, and Danny. One of them could have stolen my final. Tad was late to softball practice Monday, and Talia was late, too, getting the nachos. She said she was talking to Jeff. Any one of them had time to egg my car. Were Susan and Danny at the baseball practice? They could have done it, too. My locker could have been sprayed any time. Just because Talia was with me right before I found it doesn't mean she couldn't have done it earlier.

Kelly dried herself and changed, then wandered toward the grills. Anybody could have taken my Chem book, she thought. I left my bag lying unguarded twice that day. At lunch when I fell asleep and later, when Susan and Danny came to sit where I was.

Tad handed her a plate. "Hope you like onions," he said. "I figured if you ate them, you wouldn't notice that I had."

"Onions are fine. I thought you were going to close the grills at seven."

"That was to encourage early arrivals," Tad said. "We'll keep cooking as long as there's food left and people to eat it. Did you decide whether you were taking that job? With your father?" He set his plate on a low wall and leaned against it.

"I haven't decided," Kelly admitted, adding her plate to the top of the wall. "Did you decide on a ninety-day party or Europe?"

Tad glanced pointedly around. The seniors were laughing, shouting, and chasing each other. From the shrieks and splashes she could hear, Kelly knew people were getting tossed into the pool.

"Our future leaders," Tad said drily. "I can handle them for one night, but I don't think I could put up with this kind of fun for ninety days."

"So it's Europe?" Kelly asked.

Tad shook his head. "I thought of another option," he said. "I could stick around, maybe get a summer job, and have a summer-long private party with this charming person I met."

"Oh?" Kelly asked. "Do I know her?"

"I think so," Tad told her. "Since she was in all of your classes. She's a mechanic, too. You must know her."

"I get it," Kelly said. "But I don't get it. Guys do not all of a sudden develop incredible attractions to me. They do not propose skipping Europe to spend time with me."

"Are you telling me you're not interested?" Tad asked.

"I'm asking you why you're interested!"

Tad looked surprised. "That's a novel approach," he said. "Most people assume you should be interested in them. They think you're a little dense for not getting around to them sooner."

"This is not an approach," Kelly said. "And I'm not *most* people."

"So I noticed. Most female people aren't ace mechanics."

"I'm not an ace yet," Kelly said. "Though I will be after a couple of years in college." What am I trying to say to him? she thought, frustrated. "I'm not your type," she said finally.

"Which means you're telling me I'm not *your* type," Tad snapped. "I thought you were beyond that kind of game, Kelly. I'm not real impressed with game playing."

"Then why are you playing games with me?" Kelly asked angrily. "I feel like a bug under a microscope when I'm around you. Like a field experiment. How does the other half live? What do female mechanics say when I do this? When I say that? What are they like under the grease? What do you want with me?"

"You know what your problem is, Kelly?" Tad asked. "You're a snob. You think just because I don't have to take a summer job to pay for school, I'm a rich playboy type. You think just because I've got money I don't have anything else, like feelings. I couldn't possibly be interested in you just because you seem like an interesting person! No, I couldn't possibly have human feelings like that. I'm too rich to have ordinary feelings and be attracted to someone for ordinary reasons. Only poor people have feelings, right?"

Kelly was too astounded to answer, even when Tad strode away, leaving her alone, standing beside their two plates on the low retaining wall.

She stared at the partially eaten hamburgers, thinking, What a waste.

35

Well, I handled that with my usual finesse, Kelly thought, glancing around at the party. I'm not good at people! I was right about that.

The Sedalias' property was terraced and landscaped, with benches sheltered by tall plantings, open areas for dancing, private nooks, hedged-in gardens, paths, trees, and soft lighting over the entire closed-in area.

Kelly felt clumsy and wistful as she listened to the music, watching the couples dance. I was mean to Tad, she thought. I'm suspicious of him. Should I be? Can I accept him at face value? Tad, Talia, Jeffrey, Danny, Susan. Tad's the new one in the group. He's the one I know least well. If it has to be one of those guys, isn't he the most likely? The others could have been doing these things all along, and they weren't. If it was anyone else, why wait till now to start? This stuff started happening about the time Tad asked me to this party.

She shook her head. It's too unreal, she decided. None of those people could want to hurt me.

Eventually she realized she was watching Danny and Susan dance. Danny took Susan's hand and Kelly's hands felt cold. When Danny brushed a lock of hair from Susan's cheek, Kelly's cheek tingled.

Disgusted with herself, she turned away, watching the others instead of Danny and Susan, listening to the congratulations. I should just go home, she thought. I could take that water pump out so all I have to do tomorrow is get the new one and put it in. But I can't leave without saying good-bye to the host, and I don't really want to talk to him right now.

I was a real jerk, she decided. Tad was right. I am a snob.

"I can't believe it's over!" she heard again and again.

It is over, Kelly thought sadly. I have to go back and take more finals, so that part isn't quite over for me, but it's still over in all the other ways. It's the end of an era for us. Everyone's going to scatter, going away to college, getting married, working.

The party sounds, which had grown muted while people ate, rose again. The seniors, filled with the exhilaration of surviving finals, were loud, happy, carefree, and excited — a sharp contrast to the anxious week they'd just endured.

I'm just not in tune, Kelly thought. What did Mrs. Beckman mean I was in the right place at the right time to have stolen the test? I haven't been anywhere everyone else hasn't been, too. Where were the finals? Why was I a good suspect? Other people need good grades in English, too.

"Do you want to dance?" Tad asked, interrupting her thoughts.

Kelly turned to look at him, surprised. She felt her face heat up and knew she was blushing. "I owe you an apology," she said. "I'm sorry."

"I'm the one who's sorry," Tad said. "I have a reputation for chasing cheerleaders. I earned the reputation. I guess I even thought it was amusing. So it wasn't fair to blame you for believing my rep, not when I was the one who built it."

"Sure," Kelly said, smiling.

"Sure what?"

"I'd like to dance."

"I just happen to know there are three slow songs in a row," Tad said, moving in close to put his arms around her, holding one hand. "Right here on the tape. In my opinion, they count as one dance."

"You're pushing it," Kelly said, teasing.

"I've been thinking," Tad said.

"Hmm? About what?"

"Graduating," Tad said. "It's something we look forward to for so long, and when it gets here, it seems like it came too fast."

"I know," Kelly agreed. "It's like one minute we're kids who have to have an admit if we're late to class. The next minute we're supposed to be making decisions about college and careers like we're adults. The transition seems awfully sudden now that it's here."

"Remember I said you were a snob?" Tad asked.

"Yes," Kelly said. "You were right. I guess I did think rich people don't have the same problems the rest of us do."

"That stung. I mean, it was too true. Not that I don't have the same problems, but that I thought you didn't. I was snobbish, too, thinking your choices were easier than mine. I'm this hot-stuff top-achiever so I'm supposed to do certain things whether I want to or not. I thought it was easier for you, that you could be uncertain or afraid, could want something different from what everyone else thinks you should want. You can feel that way but I'm not supposed to. And I do."

"You mean rich kids have doubts?" Kelly asked.

Tad looked startled, but then he realized Kelly was teasing. "This rich kid does," he said. "When you said you felt like a bug under a microscope?"

"Yeah?"

"That stung, too. I used to watch you and Danny together and wonder what you both had that I didn't. You seemed so happy."

"You always seemed happy with your cheerleaders," Kelly said.

"No. We seemed appropriate together. It made the right picture. We looked like winners together."

Something tickled Kelly's brain, but she felt too good in Tad's arms to pursue it. Swaying to the music on a moonlit summer night after final exams is the definition of perfection, she thought. Or if it isn't, it should be.

"You and Danny were enjoying yourselves," Tad went on. "You were real people, having fun. I was presenting a picture, the one I thought would make my parents happy and keep my reputation intact. So when you broke up with Danny, I did tell myself exactly what you said. I decided to see how the other half lives. I thought you must know more about being happy and having fun than I did, because your life was easier than mine. I was determined to discover the secret."

"I can tell you one thing," Kelly said. "You are weird! Is it typical of rich people to be weird, or is it something you've developed on your own?"

"See?" Tad said, laughing. "You insult me and I love it. You must know more than I do about having fun. Feel free to insult me any time you like."

"Yeah, but can I touch you with greasy hands?" Kelly asked. "That's the real test."

"Try it," Tad said.

"Is that a warning or an invitation?" Kelly asked.

"Just wait and see," he told her. He held her closer, brushing her cheek with his.

Suddenly Kelly was aware that Danny was standing beside them.

"Get your hands off her!" he demanded, his voice low and threatening.

Tad looked at Kelly instead of Danny. "Does he have a say in this?" he asked.

Kelly returned Tad's earnest gaze, then looked at Danny, and beyond him, to Susan. "No," Kelly said distinctly. "He doesn't."

Susan looked momentarily hopeful and grateful, then burst into tears and ran off, toward the unlit section of the grounds beyond the party area.

36

Kelly ran after her sister, leaving Tad and Danny glaring at each other.

"Susan?" Kelly called softly. "Can I talk to you?"

Susan didn't answer, but Kelly followed the muted sounds of sobbing. As she drew nearer she could see her sister's dark form in the moonlight.

"Susan?"

"He doesn't want me," Susan said quietly. "He wants you. You always get everything you want. Everything I want, too. You're the winner. I just lose."

"Winner"? Kelly thought. That's something. . . . She moved nearer, uncertain now whether to leave or try to offer comfort. "Can I help?" she asked. "Or would it help more if I left? I know I'm not very good at things like this."

Susan made a soft noise: half sob, half hiccup. "Stay," she said.

Kelly sat on the ground near her. Susan looked so unhappy that Kelly wanted to hug her and tell her everything would be fine. She'd probably faint if I did that, Kelly decided. We don't exactly have a hugging relationship.

"Do you want him back?" Susan asked.

"I don't want to want him," Kelly answered honestly. "And I'm sure that I don't, really. Still, I guess a part of me does, whether I like it or not."

"He's like that," Susan said. "He can be such a baby. But still, there's something about him."

"Yeah, there's something about him," Kelly agreed. He's fun and charming and full of life, she thought. And I know I loved him. I guess it's not that easy to turn those feelings off after all these years, even when you know you should. Even when you want to. And then there's his temper!

Oddly, Kelly felt closer to Susan than she ever had. It's funny, she thought, but liking Danny is the first thing we've really had in common.

"I'm sorry we didn't get along, Kelly," Susan said. "I've been trying to do better."

"It shows," Kelly told her. "At first I was surprised. But I like it, Suze. I could get used to it."

"I guess I really hated you."

Hated? Kelly thought. That's too strong a word.

"Hating is so dumb!" Susan went on. "It takes so much energy. Besides, it was wasted effort. You didn't even notice."

"Oh, I noticed," Kelly said. "It was pretty obvious you didn't like me much."

"But you never reacted," Susan said. "It was like I wasn't important enough in your life to have an effect. Plus you and Dad are so close. And that made me jealous."

"I'm sorry," Kelly said.

"I'm not proud of this," Susan said quietly. "Not proud at all. But I have something to confess."

Kelly's stomach tightened. I don't want to know, she thought. "Don't say it, Susan," she said. "Whatever it is, just don't say it."

"People aren't like cars, Kelly," Susan said. "When something goes wrong in a person you can't just yank out the old motor and put a new one in."

"Engine," Kelly said tiredly. "Cars have engines, not motors."

"Whatever. You can't just buy a new engine or motor or heart or feelings. Not for people. I can't start over with you by just changing my feelings like they were . . . spark plugs. I can't just erase what happened. I have to tell you."

Kelly leaned back on her hands, looking up at the sky. The moon was so bright it faded the nearby stars, making its light and place seem the most important.

Susan followed her gaze, and evidently her thoughts, saying, "You were the moon. I was one of those little stars you can hardly see."

"That's not true," Kelly said. "You were the pretty one, the graceful, beautiful, talented daughter. You got the dance and gymnastics lessons. You got the frilly dresses, the pretty room."

"You didn't want that stuff," Susan said. "You never wanted dresses at all, and certainly not frilly ones. I didn't either. I only took them because . . . well, it was like somebody had to and I couldn't do anything else. I couldn't be like you and Dad, so I had to be what Mom picked out for me to be."

Kelly sat back up, taking the weight off her wrists. From a distance the party looked like a scene from a disorganized and very busy play, but watching, Kelly couldn't figure out the plot. The actions seemed too random to blend into a meaningful whole.

"You didn't want to get greasy," Kelly said.

"How do you know? You never asked."

She's right, Kelly thought. We presumed. Like Tad said. We presume we know what everyone else wants. What they are. What they think.

"I did want to be with you and Daddy," Susan said. "You had so much fun, laughing and wiping grease on each other, and fixing things. But when I tried to help, I wound up messing things up. I know I could have learned, but I didn't have your natural talent. So, I quit bothering you, but I resented it. Resent turns to hate pretty fast."

Like Tad again, Kelly thought. He and Susan both thought they didn't have any choices. What happens to people? Wouldn't Dad and I have taught Susan if she'd told us she wanted to learn? Or was she trying to show her interest and we just didn't understand what she was doing? Maybe all the time she was sneering at me for being greasy she was really wishing I'd include her. People! I swear cars are easier, even if Mrs. Rider's Ford did try to fool me.

Kelly sighed. "Susan," she said. "Maybe you can't just replace feelings and things. But you can rebuild them, can't you? I don't always put new parts in cars. Sometimes I just clean them up and reset them. Sometimes I file off the rough edges and replace the broken springs, and the thing works as good as new."

"I know," Susan said. "I've watched you do it. That's what I'm trying, Kelly. But first I have to do the cleaning, right? Kelly, I egged your car."

No, Kelly thought. Not Susan.

"I thought it would be funny," Susan said. She started crying. "I picked something important to you and I messed it up. I thought it would serve you right."

Kelly shook her head. "I don't want to hear any more," she said. "We'll work it out, Susan. It'll be different. Things have changed."

"That's not all," Susan said. "I squirted your locker. With Cheez-Pleez. I thought that would be funny, too."

Kelly just shook her head again.

"I didn't know how much I cared about you until you were in danger," Susan said. "When your trash can caught on fire, it was like my darkest dreams had come true. When you said you could have died I knew that was what I'd been wishing for. It was like I made it happen by wanting it to happen. It was a horrible thing to realize about myself."

Susan was crying harder. "That's what made me see how stupid I was being," she said. "I realized I didn't want you hurt after all. I felt so guilty it made me sick. That's when I really started thinking. I thought I really hated you, Kelly. But I don't. I don't hate you at all. I'm so sorry."

So am I, Kelly thought, her mind whirling. Susan did the eggs. She messed up my locker. If she was responsible, I'm safe. No one's after me.

"I'm glad you told me," she said finally. "But I can't handle hearing any more right now. I need time to think. Susan, I don't hate you. I never did. I think I'm going to be furious about this once I've had time to think about it, but for right now I'm too overwhelmed to talk anymore. Okay?"

Susan nodded, wiping her cheeks with her hands.

How could I be so stupid? Kelly wondered. The enemy was in my own house! All I had to do was talk with her, pay attention to her, and I wouldn't have had an enemy at all. How could I be so blind? What else have I been blind about?

A tiny flicker of hope made Kelly raise her head and scan the distant party again, this time looking for Talia.

37

Kelly found Tad first, sitting on the low wall alone, watching the couples dancing.

"You're not bleeding," Kelly said. "Does that mean Danny is?"

"Why would he be bleeding?" Tad asked, looking surprised.

Kelly frowned. "Didn't I run off after Susan, and leave you two glaring at each other?"

"We were disagreeing," Tad admitted. "That doesn't mean blood, though, Kelly."

"It does with Danny," she said.

Tad laughed. "Danny and I fought once," he said. "In the ninth grade. We both had bloody faces and loose teeth and sore knuckles, and we both lost. Or both won. It was a draw, anyway. We agreed to quit fighting while we could both still move. I don't think either one of us was eager to try it again tonight. We discussed our problem, Kelly."

"That doesn't sound like the Danny I know," Kelly insisted. "Are you sure you don't have him mixed up with someone else?"

"Come here," Tad said, holding out a hand. "I'll prove it."

Puzzled, Kelly took his hand, and he led her around the corner of the house, to a more private, dimmer place. He stopped and put his arms around her.

"How does this prove you didn't have Danny confused with someone else?" Kelly asked.

Tad didn't answer. Instead, he bent down and kissed her, his hands gently rubbing her shoulders.

He kisses softer than Danny does, Kelly thought.

She smiled at Tad. "I still don't see how that proves anything about Danny."

Tad grinned. "You will," he said. "Danny wants to talk with you, Kelly. He thinks you still love him. And I think you aren't really sure."

He took her hand again, and they headed slowly back the way they had come. "I figured," he went on, "if you were going to have to vote, it should be an informed vote. I wanted you to have something to remember when I sent you to talk with Danny."

Tad stopped as they rounded the corner again. He nodded toward the steps that led inside to the pool. "He's in the game room. It's to the right of the changing rooms. It's your decision, Kelly. I think we could have something special, but not as long as you have any doubts about Danny."

"You're sending me off to make a choice?" Kelly asked. "I don't believe this. I was looking for Talia."

"She's looking for you, too. So is Jeff. I guess his car broke down on the way here and they want you to take a look at it. But they'll wait. You need to talk with Danny first. And make your decision."

Kelly gave him a stubborn look. "I didn't come here tonight to make choices," she said. "And I don't like other people deciding what I need to do and who I need to talk to. I'm not in the mood to talk to Danny. I'm not in the mood to have a choice forced on me. I want to find Talia."

"She's out by the Japanese gardens," Tad said. "But Kelly . . ."

Kelly remembered passing a Japanese-style bridge when she'd run after Susan so she headed that way again, leaving Tad looking surprised at her desertion.

"There you are!" Talia said. "I've been looking all over for you since you got out of the pool. Where have you been hiding?"

"Around," Kelly said. It's a long story, she thought.

Talia had found a little pagoda-like picnic area and was sitting on a bench behind a table inside, facing Tad's house so she could watch the party. Kelly sat on the other bench across from her.

"I'm really very angry with you," Talia said.

"You don't sound angry," Kelly told her. "Are you really? Or are you teasing?"

"Mostly really," Talia said.

"Then yell at me," Kelly told her.

Talia didn't say anything right away.

"It's better to just go ahead and get it out," Kelly said, thinking of Susan. She kept it inside for years, she thought. And it was poisonous.

"I don't know," Talia said finally. "I've been waiting and waiting for your tests to be over so you'd return to some semblance of normal. I figured tonight would be a good time, but tonight finally got here and not only are you not done with your finals, you've been ignoring me. How many finals do you have to take over?"

"Spanish and Chemistry. Plus Computer Lit, I guess."

"So are you still a nervous wreck?"

"I don't think so," Kelly said, surprised to realize it was true.

"You don't realize how crazy you get," Talia said. "For two months ahead of time all you could think about was cars and finals. You were obsessed, Kel. I'm surprised you haven't chewed your fingernails off clear up to your knuckles."

"I didn't know I was that bad. I'm sorry. I did know you've had something on your mind, but you wouldn't talk about it. You've been peculiar, too."

"It's the same old question, that's all," Talia said. "What to do after graduation."

"You applied to Dartmouth, with Jeffrey," Kelly said. "You told me you got accepted."

"No, I didn't. You just assumed I got accepted. I did get accepted to some other colleges, but not Dartmouth. My grades aren't good enough, especially in Math and Science."

"I'm sorry," Kelly told her.

"Me, too. I don't want to go to the other schools when Jeff will be at Dartmouth. And I didn't want to bother you with my problems. You were too worried about your own."

"Oh, Talia!" Kelly said, shaking her head. "And I didn't even ask! What kind of friend am I, anyway?"

"You asked if I was okay," Talia said. "All the time, in fact."

"But I knew you weren't. And I didn't do anything about it. I should have come over and put on some old records until you started getting nostalgic."

"Then I'd have cried," Talia said, trying to smile.

"And then you would have talked. I know how to get you to open up. I just didn't do it. And I'm sorry."

"I wish you had," Talia said, a note of depression coloring her voice. "Because I'm afraid I didn't handle things very well on my own. You would have made me see how desperate I was acting."

"What?" Kelly asked. "Tee, what did you do?"

38

"I'm not like you, Kelly. I'm not strong and confident. I'm not skilled. I'm not independent. I could have decided to go to a small school and train for something. But I didn't want to go alone. I wanted to be with Jeffrey. And I kept thinking of all those dull classes and all those smart people who'd be better than I was at everything."

Kelly sighed. It's the no-choices problem, again, she thought. She decided she didn't have any options.

"I got scared," Talia said. "I'm afraid of being a nobody. A loser. I told Jeffrey he should use his tuition money and get an apartment and we could get married. I figured he could go to a cheaper college, and we could use the extra money for the apartment."

Kelly sighed again.

"I know. Dumb idea," Talia said. "And Jeffrey's pretty excited about getting into Dartmouth. His father went there, too. Jeff's got a real chance to make something of himself, and he wouldn't give that up for anything, not even me. But he did like the idea of getting married."

Kelly sighed again.

"I know," Talia said. "We kept talking it over and coming up with all kinds of ideas. We finally decided I should get a job near Dartmouth and find us a place to live. We'd get married secretly and Jeff would go ahead and go to college."

"Why would it have to be a secret that you were married?" Kelly asked. "There's something wrong when you have to keep secrets about big things like that."

Talia took a deep breath and let it out slowly. "We couldn't afford to live on my salary," she said. "What I was going to do was tell my parents I was going to Blake. That's a little business college about forty miles from Dartmouth. Then I was going to use the money they gave me for tuition and room to pay for the apartment."

"Oh, Talia!" Kelly said. "You know you wouldn't be happy like that! You'd hate it that you were tricking your parents and lying to them. You'd be miserable, and then you'd start resenting Jeff and hating him for being a part of it."

"Where were you yesterday?" Talia asked softly. "When I was coming to the very same conclusion? I can't do it, Kelly. And I don't know how to tell Jeff. It was my idea, really. I talked Jeff into it. But now he's even more excited about it than I was. All I wanted was to be a winner at something, and look at the mess I made!"

Kelly reached across the table and took Talia's

hands in hers. They were cold and Kelly rubbed them. "I wasn't there when you needed me," Kelly said. "There's nothing I can do about that. But I'm here now, Talia. I won't let you down this time. You can tell Jeff. He'll understand. He might not be happy at first, but if he loves you, he'll get used to the idea. No one wants to sneak and lie, Talia. Jeff doesn't, either, and he'll realize you're right."

Talia gave her a small smile. "Do you have a tissue?" she asked.

"No. Sorry. Should I go get you some?"

"Not yet. I don't want you to leave yet."

"Was there something else you wanted to tell me?" Kelly asked. "About me being childish about my hat?"

Talia looked puzzled. "I never thought you were childish about your hat. I liked your hat."

"You didn't tell Jeffrey that you never saw such childish behavior and you'd had just about enough and you were going to tell me so?"

"I guess you are still a little crazy," Talia said. "Those makeup finals must be getting to you more than you thought. I swear I never said or thought that you . . . wait a minute. I did say that about Susan."

"Susan?"

"You mean you missed that?" Talia asked. "The first time in history Susan stuck up for you and you missed it? It was pretty impressive, believe me! Susan doesn't do anything halfway. Kelly, I can't believe no one mentioned that to you!"

"Well, what happened?"

"Susan started accusing everyone, I guess. Your hat disappeared sixth period, and evidently Susan spent sixth and seventh period trying to search everyone's cars and get up a search party to check out all the lockers and bathrooms and the locker rooms. When Jeff and I left after school she was in the front hall calling people names because they wouldn't help her look. She threw an absolute fit!"

Kelly grinned, thinking how wound up Susan could get. "I missed it totally," she said. "I walked out of Chem class, out of the school the back way, and went home."

"I wish you'd seen it," Talia said. "It was a doozy. Everybody just walked off, finally. Left her there, yelling. I guess eventually she shut up. I was glad she wanted to help you, Kelly, but she just didn't know how to do it. She was creating more of a problem by yelling and wanting to search everyone. That didn't solve anything. I'm sure people would have helped look if she hadn't been so obnoxious, and it made me mad to see her ruining things again."

Kelly burst out laughing. She didn't know which she was laughing at more — the image of Susan yelling to nobody about Kelly's missing hat, or the fact that she'd been so stupid about Talia.

Kelly stood up and hugged Talia across the table. "You're a peach!" she said happily.

"A peach?" Talia repeated. "Red and yellow and fuzzy? I'm flattered, Kelly."

"And I'm an idiot," Kelly said. "Talia, it was Susan who squirted the Cheez-Pleez into my locker and did all that stuff. She just wanted me to recognize her as a person. To include her. To believe she was important. I ignored her, and I ignored you. I've been a real idiot."

"Susan? Did she steal your Spanish test? And trash your room? And egg your car?"

"Well, she told me about the eggs. It never would have happened if I hadn't been so caught up in my own miseries. I was selfish. I promise to try not to be that way anymore. If I do, will you knock me on the head a few times to get my attention?"

"I'd love to," Talia said.

They sat quietly for a few minutes, enjoying each other's presence. Then Talia said, "Kelly, remember I told you Jeff's car was acting up?"

"Yeah. I heard you guys had some trouble."

"It broke down," Talia told her. "Jeff insisted it was fine, and he took me for a long drive before the party, talking about our plans and all. And the darned car just chug-chugged to a stop. Jeff tried to start it for a long time, until the battery wouldn't do anything but whine at us."

"Where?"

"I don't know. Back up this windy little road. We had to walk a couple of miles before some old guy gave us a ride in his pickup truck."

"You know I'll be glad to go take a look at it," Kelly said. "But I don't have the things with me to fix it. I have tools, but if anything needs to be replaced, I don't have the parts."

"You carry spares for your car. Won't anything fit?"

Kelly shrugged. "They might do in an emergency," she said. "If the plugs are fouled, mine would fit his car size-wise. They're not really hot enough for his engine, but I suppose they'd get him down out of the hills without having to call a tow truck."

"Kelly, I want you to do me a favor," Talia said. "I want you to take Jeffrey to get his car and take a long time doing it. I need at least an hour without him so I can figure out a way to tell him I've changed my mind."

"Where is he now?" Kelly asked.

"He was playing Ping-Pong with Danny in the game room last I saw. I kind of sneaked out. I bet he's looking for me by now. So he could be anywhere. I'm just not ready to face him yet, Kel. I need a little time to work up to it. I want to convince him I mean it, but I don't want to lose him."

"Okay," Kelly said. "I'll see if I can track him down."

39

Kelly set off across the lawn, thinking how easy it was to assume that no one else had problems when you were lost in your own.

Susan was pretty, Kelly thought. And spoiled. That's all I saw. I didn't see that she was hurting. People do have symptoms. They may be a little harder to recognize than a car's, but they're there. And a little preventive maintenance goes a long way. I ignored everybody too long. If I ignored my car like that it'd fall apart. I should have realized people need a little loving care, too. There I was, being suspicious of everyone because they were acting odd, and they were acting odd because I wasn't paying attention to them.

She stopped halfway across the lawn, her eyes moving slowly over the groups of people, seeking Jeffrey.

Wait a minute, she thought. The fire was Wednesday night. Susan didn't say she started the fire; she just said it was *like* it was her fault. And it was the fire that made her start thinking. But my Chem book was taken some time Thursday. I know it was. I studied from it during my free classes that morning.

And my hat. That disappeared Thursday, too. Susan was supposedly already on my side by then. And besides, she had that fit about it being gone. That doesn't sound like something she'd do if she'd taken it. And I took Mrs. Rider's car apart Thursday. I spent most of the evening doing it, in fact. My hat wasn't there then, so it had to be put under the car later.

Kelly went on slowly, thinking, no longer looking for Jeffrey in the crowds of seniors. Either Susan kept on doing things to me after she said she stopped . . . or I don't have the whole story yet.

When Kelly drew near the dance Tad joined her. "It worked last time we argued," he said. "Maybe it'll work again."

"Maybe what will?" Kelly asked.

"Dancing. Will you dance with me?"

"It could be you," Kelly said, studying his face as if hoping she could see guilt or innocence written there.

"What could be me?"

"You could be the one who's after me," Kelly said.

Tad grinned. "Of course I'm after you," he said. "I haven't made any secret of it, have I? Do you want to dance or just stand there staring at me?"

"I haven't had my turn yet," came Danny's voice from behind Kelly. "That was our agreement, if you remember. I'd really appreciate it, Kelly," he added.

"One dance," Kelly said. "Then I have to find Jeffrey so we can go take a look at his car."

Tad didn't look pleased, but he moved aside and watched while Danny put his arms around Kelly.

"It's been too long since I held you," Danny told her. "The last time I tried I got mad. Punched your locker."

"I remember," Kelly said.

"You may not always be able to tell, but I value your advice." Danny grinned. "I'm working very hard on my temper. I'm trying two old, time-tested tricks that my grandmother suggested."

"What?"

"Counting to ten, and walking away," Danny said. "Both techniques help a lot."

"I'm glad," Kelly said. "I was impressed that you had a discussion with Tad. In fact, I was amazed."

"Instead of punching his face in, you mean?" Danny grinned again. "I wanted to. When I saw him with his arms around you I had to count to 200."

Kelly laughed, but sobered as Danny's arms tightened their hold. "Danny," she said softly. "You'd better get used to counting."

Danny let his arms fall to his sides as the music ended. "You're choosing him? He's going to be the winner?"

Kelly felt a warning tickle at her brain again. She frowned. It's that darned little book, she thought.

Winners. But it was just a book. It wasn't anything important. "I'm not choosing anybody," she said. "I don't have to. I already broke up with you. That hasn't changed. It's final, Danny. But that doesn't mean I'm choosing Tad. I hardly know him. I like him, and I'd like to get to know him, and that's all I'm choosing. To get to know someone who seems like a nice guy."

It could be Danny, too, she thought. It has to be someone who was in the Spanish class because the teacher would have remembered if anyone else had come in.

"I've got to check Jeff's car," Kelly told Danny. "See if I can get it running long enough to get it home."

"Are you going home afterward? Is this good night?"

"No, I'll be back."

"Can I have the last dance?" Danny asked.

"You can have one more dance," Kelly said. "But not the last one, Danny. That's for your date. And mine."

"They could dance together," Danny suggested hopefully.

Kelly grinned, shaking her head. "You never give up, do you?"

40

Kelly found Jeffrey looking for Talia by the Japanese gardens.

"Have you seen her?" he asked. "I seem to have lost her."

"She sent me to find you," Kelly said. "We're supposed to go fetch the car."

"Oh. Is Talia coming, too?"

"No," Kelly said. "She asked me to go check it out with you. She isn't crazy about watching engine repairs, and there's no reason she should miss the party. This may be the last time we're all together, other than graduation. We can handle the job ourselves."

"I suppose," Jeff said. "Though I haven't seen her that much, myself, tonight. It would have been nice to have the company."

"Tell me about the car," Kelly suggested, starting toward the parking lot. "Talia told me it was chugging and whining. That's not a very helpful description."

Jeffrey fell into step beside her. "It acted like it

wasn't getting enough gas," he said. "But always before when it did that, it only lasted a few seconds and then cut back in again. It only actually died once before, and I got it started again right away. This time it wouldn't start at all."

"It would turn over but not catch?" Kelly asked.

"It turned over fine until I wore the battery down."

"When's the last time you had it tuned?"

Jeffrey gave her a shamefaced smile. "I don't remember," he said.

"You don't remember when, or you don't remember ever?" Kelly asked.

"Ever," he admitted. "I thought it was a self-tuning model."

"Too bad there's no such thing," Kelly said, laughing. "You got it the beginning of last year, right?"

"Just before Halloween. It cost me 142 brooms in trade-in."

Kelly unlocked the T-bird and they got in. "So it's overdue for a tune-up," she said, starting the car. "Actually, that's hopeful. Which direction?"

"Right. Why is that hopeful?"

"If you've never had it tuned, chances are that's all it is. A fouled plug or two. A loose belt. A terribly dirty filter. Poor choke adjustment or stuck choke. Something easy."

"Oh, good. I vote for easy."

"But if it's not something easy, you'll have to get it towed," Kelly warned. "You'll have to have it looked at in daylight. The problems get tougher after we eliminate tune-up stuff. Coil, alternator, timing chain. The distributor bushings. Even an electrical problem, though if it's the pickup coil it wouldn't even turn over. We'd have to have the parts to get those things fixed."

"Turn onto the highway," Jeffrey directed. "Take exit 244. I really appreciate you doing this, Kelly. I feel pretty stupid. Talia told me to have you look at it last week. It's just, with finals and all, it didn't seem that important. Come to think of it, eating and breathing didn't seem that important, either."

"I know," Kelly said. "It's no problem looking at it, Jeff. I'm a mechanic. I like looking at cars."

"I never knew a mechanic who made house calls," Jeff said. "Uh-oh, does that mean you charge as much as doctors do when they make house calls?"

"No charge for the rescue," Kelly said, laughing. "But if we have to tow it back and do something major, then I'll charge."

"You need a business manager," Jeff said. "You're never supposed to work for free. You'll never get rich that way. You've got to charge for everything, starting with the next job."

"Who cares about rich?" Kelly asked. "Right now all I need is enough for tuition and tools. Maybe I'll raise my rates when I move to my own place. I'll have more expenses then."

A little later Kelly took the exit, turning left at Jeff's direction. The road was narrow and winding, with poorly patched potholes and heave cracks, with only a faint yellow line marking the center.

They climbed steadily, doubling back around a few hairpin curves.

"What were you doing up here?" Kelly asked.

"Oh, just looking," Jeff said.

"I'll bet it's pretty in the daylight," Kelly said, maneuvering between two holes. "The road isn't very good for your alignment, though. Or your suspension."

"I found a real nice spot," Jeff said. "Not too far from here, in fact. Luckily the car stalled in the only place along here with a wide shoulder. You'll be able to pull off."

"Good. How much farther?"

"I don't know, exactly. Maybe a mile or two. It looks different at night."

They rode in silence for a while, Kelly driving slowly, carefully avoiding potholes and watching for the disabled car. I'd hate to find it by running into it, she thought.

"Um . . . Kelly?" Jeff sounded hesitant.

"Yeah?"

"I don't know how to say this."

"Just do it," Kelly suggested. "If there's one thing I've learned this week, I learned it's better to just say it."

"Well . . . how well do you know Tad?"

"Not very," Kelly admitted. "We aren't exactly from the same social circles. Why?"

"It's probably none of my business," Jeff said slowly. "But you're a good friend of Talia's. It just doesn't seem right to not say anything at all."

"So say it," Kelly told him.

"He's changed," Jeff said. "He's not the same person he was a year ago. He worries me a little. He's . . . unpredictable. There's nothing I can really pinpoint, Kelly, but things like in Phys Ed he started taking cheap shots at people. Things that could be accidents, like when we're playing and he falls on someone's knee. He always apologizes, but he'll seem . . . happy about it."

"There's the car," Kelly said, cutting across the road and easing to a stop. "Go on, Jeff. I'm listening."

Jeff unlocked his car and popped the hood. The moonlight shone brightly on the car, casting deep shadows beneath the hood, highlighting the air filter cover, the battery, the coil.

"Once or twice, you'd expect," Jeff said. "People have accidents. They get wrapped up in a game and forget to watch out. But it's been happening a lot. It got so we all just keep away from him as much as we can. Should I try to start it?"

"Yeah, go ahead." Kelly listened to the click from the battery. "It's dead," she said. "I can't tell anything till we jump it. But let me get the droplight. We'll check a few things first."

Kelly plugged the light into her cigarette lighter and stretched the cord to Jeff's car, hanging the light from his hood, adjusting it to brighten the shadows.

"Like I said," Jeff went on. "There's nothing I can really pinpoint, but that business in Phys Ed is mean. And he's moody these days, too. Like he's got some kind of problem he can't deal with. I suppose it's tough being the perfect everything. If you've seen his father, you know what I mean. I wouldn't even have mentioned it except you're Talia's friend. I guess what I'm saying is, I feel creepy around him, sometimes. So that's it. I told you I didn't know how to say it."

"I appreciate the warning," Kelly said. "Your battery fluid's low, Jeff. We'd better fill it before we jump it." She got a gallon of water from the T-bird's trunk, filled the battery cells, and popped the plastic caps back on. She pulled the cables and scraped the inside curve, checked for corrosion on the posts. The connections looked clean.

"Try it again." Is it true? she wondered. About Tad? His father did seem as if he could be hard to get along with.

The battery made a groaning effort. "Okay, stop," Kelly called.

She hooked up the jumper cables and started her car. "Now try," she told Jeff. Could Tad be deliberately mean? Jeff sees him in situations I don't, like in gym class.

Jeff turned the key, holding it on. The battery's efforts began to sound more impressive, but the car didn't start. Kelly checked the choke, but it wasn't stuck. It seemed to be operating as it should.

"Stop," she called. The belts are fine, she thought, testing.

"I'm going to pull a plug," she told Jeff. I guess I'll take his opinion as a caution, she decided. And watch. I was planning to be cautious and careful with Tad, anyway.

She turned her car off, grabbed some tools, disconnected the jumper cables, and bent over the engine compartment, pulling the wire from the closest plug. Jeff looked on.

"Maybe he's just under a lot of pressure," Jeff said. "From his father. They always want you to do better than they did. To get better grades, do better in sports, get a better education. And they don't want you to make the same mistakes they did. In fact, they don't want you to make any mistakes at all."

"Plug's fine," Kelly muttered. She scraped it, checked the gap, then reinserted it, starting it by hand, then putting the wrench on. I'll try another one, she decided. On the other side. He's only got six, so each one counts. I just can't picture Tad being mean. He's too thoughtful. And he didn't fight with Danny, even though he had the chance.

"They don't seem to understand that we're different," Jeff said.

"Who?" Kelly asked.

"Fathers. I'm not him. I'm not even as good as he was. How could I possibly be better? I keep trying. Everything he says to do, I do."

Jeff lapsed into silence, watching while Kelly checked the rest of the plugs, the fuel and air filters, the points.

"I think it's the distributor, Jeff," Kelly said finally. "I've checked everything else. Your wiring seems fine, and so does everything else. Maybe the bushings. I can't do anything about that here. I need to work on it at home where I can check things out more thoroughly."

"Do you mean you're giving up?" Jeff asked.

Kelly laughed. "I mean I checked everything I can check while we're parked out here in the middle of the night in the middle of nowhere with not very many tools and poor light," she said. "You're going to have to get it towed. To my place if you want me to do the work, to another garage if you want someone else to do it."

"You never get anywhere quitting," Jeff said.

"Does that mean I'm hired?" Kelly asked. "I'm perfectly willing to keep going, but not here. I need daylight and tools."

She coiled the jumper cables and put them in the T-bird's trunk, gathered her tools, and started wiping them with a rag.

"Are you sure you checked everything?" Jeff asked.

Kelly gave him a disgusted look. This is no longer amusing, she thought. Would he ask that at a shop? If the mechanic was a guy? Here I am, doing him a favor, and he's griping?

"Maybe you want someone else to check it out," she said. She plunked the toolbox in the trunk, unplugged the droplight.

"I just can't believe you're giving up!" Jeff said. "The car was working almost fine. It can't be anything very serious or it would have given me more trouble all along."

Kelly put the droplight away and closed her trunk. She checked for leftover tools, feeling under Jeff's hood before she closed it. She hadn't actually worked on the T-bird, but the habit of checking for forgotten tools and parts was so ingrained that she felt around beneath her own hood, checking the rim that ran across the front of the engine compartment, and the top of the air cleaner — the places she habitually set tools and bolts while she was working.

"I'm very disappointed in you," Jeff said. He locked his car door, slammed it shut. "For quitting."

This is just a little strange, Kelly thought uneasily.

"A quitter never wins," Jeff said, heading for the T-bird.

Kelly, guided only by a slight, sudden chill, reached out casually and yanked the Thunderbird's fuel line free at the carburetor. I can always put it back, she thought.

"And a winner never quits," Jeff said. "I remembered."

Winners? Kelly thought. The little book? It's Jeff's book? Movement in the storage room. A noise. Jeff dropped the book? From where? If it fell, it must have been up . . . but how? I didn't see anyone. Where was he?

She froze, her mind and body locked. *In the right place at the right time*, she remembered Mrs. Beckman saying. *To have stolen the test.*

Does that mean . . . ?

41

Jeff's hand clamped on her arm, just above her elbow, his fingers digging painfully into her muscles.

Too late, she thought. I should have run while I had the chance.

He jerked her back from the T-bird, slamming the hood shut. He yanked her to the driver's side and shoved her in. "Get over," he said, climbing in behind her, pushing her over the console. "I'm driving now." He dangled the keys briefly, then realized there were keys still in the ignition. He dropped the spares on the floor and started the car.

My spare set, Kelly thought, surprised, but only dully so. He's the one who took my purse. Of course. Jeff?

"Four point three miles up the road," Jeffrey muttered. "A nice place. I found it."

He stole the copy of the English final. Kelly felt despair as she realized the truth. It's been Jeffrey all along. But how could he? Susan did my locker, egged my car . . . and Jeff did everything else? Why? I wouldn't have told on him, even if I'd known.

He held her arm so tightly it felt heavy, throbbing. He was cutting off the circulation. Kelly kept herself still, breathing slowly, trying to gather her thoughts and energy, trying to find confidence or courage or even an idea. Jeff had pulled out onto the wrong side of the road, driving in the left-hand lane.

"Where is my *Winners*?" Jeff asked, shaking her captive arm.

The car won't go for long, Kelly told herself. I pulled the fuel line. Be ready.

She leaned toward Jeff.

"Where is it? I saw you take it. I want it back and I won't quit till I get it because *a winner never quits*. I remember."

"Why, Jeff?" Kelly asked.

"There's only one number one. And that's me. I'm the winner. Just me. Nobody ever said winning would be easy, son. It takes guts. It takes blood." Jeff gave an old laugh. "I thought he meant *my* blood. I had it all wrong, but I'll fix it. I'll do it right this time."

He finally pulled over into the right-hand lane. "Where is it?" he asked. "Where's my *Winners*? Where?"

Kelly leaned still closer to Jeff, almost listening as she waited for the Thunderbird to stall. She felt the first hesitancy. "I burned it!" she shouted. The car lurched as the gas emptied from the carburetor. As it lurched, as she shouted, Kelly yanked the door open and threw herself to the right, the momentum as she fell wrenching her arm free of Jeff's grip.

She gasped as she hit the ground, trying to roll with the force. She regained her feet, crying out softly at the pain in her hip and shoulder from landing. She set off in a limping run, not waiting to see what Jeff did.

Stupid! she thought. I should have run earlier. I froze. I should have figured it out earlier. I should have found out whose book it was. Dumb. I am so dumb! Why? Why was Jeff trying to hurt me? Because of a book?

The moon lit the landscape, making Kelly feel exposed and vulnerable. The boulders and low bushes near the road didn't offer much shelter. Beyond them the land rose sharply, the covering of bushes thickening, with a few dense stands of trees. But uphill was also the direction away from the car. Running was no more than a temporary escape, to gain time. The car was the only real way out.

Over the pounding of her heart, the gasp of her breath, and the blood pulsing in her ears Kelly could hear the rhythmic sound of footsteps pursuing her. Too close, she thought, pouring on a desperate effort. Too close. I can't get away.

She dodged a boulder, running for the nearest copse of trees, knowing she wasn't fast enough, and that even if she could make the trees, they would offer no protection.

Jeff ran right over the boulder and leaped on her from behind, tumbling her to the ground and knocking the breath out of her lungs.

Kelly couldn't breathe but still she tried to fight, her efforts seeming feeble even to herself. They had no effect on Jeff at all. He knocked her arms aside and grabbed her, grunting. As he heaved her up Kelly got her wind back. She gasped as he tossed her over his shoulder, the hard shoulder bone digging into her stomach.

Kelly fought nausea, kicking and squirming.

"Stop it!" Jeff said, his voice low and commanding.

Kelly kicked harder. Jeff stopped suddenly and slammed her to the ground, shouting, "Quit moving!"

The blow of landing rocked her, snapping her head back and short-circuiting all the message-sending synapses in her brain. She was not unconscious, yet the clarity of her mind wouldn't translate into control over her limbs.

She couldn't move as Jeff picked her up again, couldn't squirm or kick. She couldn't even think. She was simply aware — mostly of the roughness of Jeffrey's gait, the unpleasant jerking up and down as he carried her back over the landscape she'd run across to get away from him, and the unanswered question, Why?

Then she was aware of sound. The crunch, crunch of Jeffrey's feet, his labored breaths, his low chanting, his voice almost singsong.

"Hard," he said. "Heavy. She's heavy, Dad. But I won't drop her. Only if I want to, but not by accident. I can do it. I'll keep going forever and never quit. I'm a winner, Dad. You'll see. I'll be the best. Just for you."

Then feeling returned to her body, and Kelly

groaned, biting back a scream of pain.

"I had a good place picked out," Jeff crooned. "A good one. Steep. Toss you right over. Push the T-bird over. Can't do that now. I wanted *Winners* back. That was all. But it wasn't in the car. Eggs were. Eggs were in the car, but not *Winners*. Cheese in the locker, but not *Winners*. Not in the purse. Not in the bedroom. I couldn't let her have my secrets. Now she's burned them. I thought I burned her, but she came back to trick me. But I'm going to be a winner anyway. There's only one best and she can't be it. I have to be."

Kelly felt like a rag doll, limp and lifeless. Every step Jeff took jounced through her, sending stabs of pain that throbbed as the next stab sliced her.

I have to do something, she thought. But what? What can I do? It's another final exam . . . the ultimate final. If I lose, I die. He really plans to kill me. I have to do something, but what? I can't think of a plan. I have to think.

Jeff stopped suddenly, letting her slide to the ground. Kelly felt herself begin to faint as she hit, but the blackness receded slowly, leaving her light-headed, too dizzy to move.

"It's not very steep here," Jeff said, his words labored. "Not as nice as the other place. But it'll do. And I can push the car over here from across the road. It's not far."

"Why?" Kelly croaked.

Jeff looked at her, surprised. "I was going to die," he said. "When you told everyone. I would be ruined, and that would kill me. I saw it all, Kelly, and it was awful! Being a dead failure. You wouldn't believe how much it hurt! I couldn't go to Dad's college anymore and he was disappointed. He only wants me when I'm a winner. I have to be a winner. When you stood up there and told everyone what I had done, it killed me."

He isn't making sense, Kelly thought. Told who? I didn't tell anybody anything. I didn't figure it out until it was too late.

She tried moving, watching his face. Her body felt broken and bruised, battered, but it moved. She pulled her legs beneath her, slowly.

"You had my *Winners*," Jeff said. His breathing had slowed but his voice still sounded odd, still had an edge of the singsong lilt. "I was having trouble remembering how to win, but I had to. I had to win. You wouldn't give me *Winners* back and I couldn't find it. You and the principal made traps but I was too smart. I bet you thought I didn't know what you were doing, but I figured it out. I was too smart. I didn't fall in any traps. None of them."

Kelly didn't think she could make the effort of leaping to her feet and rushing him, but she knew she had to at least stand. It was still hard to breathe. She could only take shallow breaths and even then, it seemed that a bone grated in her chest with each breath, sending jabs of agony through her.

Slowly she moved her arms, maneuvering them into position to push herself up.

"Stop!" Jeff ordered. "I have to push you now. I have to. I cannot stray from the path. I remember that." He leaned toward her, arms outstretched.

"I didn't really burn it," Kelly said.

Jeff stopped, as frozen as Kelly had been earlier. "Give it to me," he said, hissing the words.

"I have to stand up," Kelly said. "To get it from my pocket."

She rolled slowly to her feet, ignoring the aching protest the movement set into gear. As she stood, she pulled her right hand to her chest, cupped it slightly, and then lashed out at Jeffrey's throat. The blow connected solidly with his flesh but Kelly couldn't tell what she'd hit.

He bent forward at the waist, making choking noises.

Kelly ran for her car, gasping in pain. She felt like she was trying to run underwater and the waves crashing against her were waves of pain. Finally she reached the Thunderbird. Jeff had left it where it had stalled, half off the road, half in the traffic lane.

Kelly fumbled with the hood release latch, felt it give, pulled the hood up. She knew she could find the gas line in the dark, replace it by feel . . . if she just had enough time.

Jeff's hands closed around her neck, and he yanked her backward, dragging her across the road again. "I'll do it, Daddy!" he shouted in a chilling, little-boy voice. "I'll never give up. Are you proud now? Are you proud of me?"

Kelly struggled. She tried to kick, to gouge, to damage him anywhere, anyhow. The pain and fear melted together, becoming one black thing inside as Jeffrey heaved her over the cliff.

42

The blackness engulfed her this time, wrapping her, soothing the edges of the terror. Unthinkingly, Kelly grabbed at the air, reflexively seeking a handhold, a lifeline, anything to slow the mad tumble, the sickening bottomlessness of falling, crashing against sharp things, rolling, rolling toward death.

And then she stopped, wedged uncomfortably against something hard-edged and jagged, aching, certain she was totally smashed, but obviously alive.

She opened her eyes. There was no sign of Jeffrey above her, looking to make sure she was dead.

She glanced around. She had come to rest against a rock, which was embedded in the earth at the foot of a large, thorny bush that grew about halfway down the slope. The slope itself was dotted with rocky outcroppings, bushes, and a weedlike covering of plants.

Kelly struggled to her knees, still looking around, hoping something would set off a chain reaction of thought that would gel into a plan.

Should I stay here? Move? Climb up? What if he comes down to finish me off? I'd better not be here. What if he starts rolling big rocks down the hill? Could I possibly dodge them? I can't move that fast. But I'd better move. I can't be where he expects me to be.

The slope above her was steep, but not quite the sheer sides of an actual cliff. She wondered what the spot was like that he had originally chosen to throw her over, and shuddered, glad he had tossed her over here, instead, where she had a chance of surviving . . . if he wasn't already pushing the T-bird toward the same spot so it would roll down over her.

That thought gave her the push she needed to move, and she set off at an angle, knowing she couldn't climb up at the same place she'd fallen in case the T-bird came crashing down, yet knowing, too, that she didn't have the strength to go very far out of the way.

Her arms ached, yet she forced them to reach out and grab clumps of grass, using the grass to pull against, to get herself started upward. Her legs cooperated reluctantly, the muscles bunching, pushing her upward.

The slope steepened about halfway up, leading to the almost-undercut section right before the top, and Kelly needed the help of every handhold she found. Her chest still sent sharp messages with each breath. The top of the hill seemed too far away.

I can't make it, Kelly thought. It's too far up. How can I climb that far when I can barely move?

This is just like climbing the ropes in Phys Ed. Did I flunk that final, too? No, I got an A. Why do I have to take the test again? Up. Pull up.

Her arms felt like weights. To the top, she thought tiredly. I have to keep doing this over and over forever until I get it right. What if someone is up there with a knife, sawing at the rope? No, it's not a rope, it's a car, my car. He's going to push my car over, too, so it will crash down on me and flatten me like a bug. If I'm going to fall, I'm going to fall from the top. Jeffrey's up there, and he'll never quit. Winners never quit. He'll stomp on my fingers when I get there.

When I get there, she repeated. I'm more than halfway. I'll get there. I got an A. Reach up. Grab ahold. Pull. Just do it, Kelly.

The steeper section at the top seemed impossible till she realized there was a root to grab hold of, a root that shone white and bonelike in the moonlight, but that held when Kelly tested it. She hauled herself up more, on and on, by root and clump until she was almost to the top. She stopped climbing, resting, letting her breath slow, trying to listen for the T-bird's wheels as Jeff pushed it toward her, trying to hear whether she was far enough to the side so the car would miss her.

My T-bird, she thought sadly. So beautiful. He's going to ruin it. Smashed, crashed, just like him. Tangled and twisted, poor beautiful things. She started weeping silently and didn't know whether she cried for Jeffrey or her car. Or both of them.

I'm not done, she reminded herself. It's never

going to be over. I have to reach the top. Whatever is up there, I have to keep going.

She reached out for another root, grabbed, pulled to test it. It broke off in her fist and she sobbed. She heard an echo of her sob from above her, to her left. Confused, she forced her feet to dig into the side of the earth wall, giving her a foothold until she could grab a bigger root.

It held. She hauled herself up the last few feet, heaved her upper body over the edge, crying out softly in spite of herself as her sore ribs hit the ground. Her legs dangled below her but she didn't want to put out the effort it would take to heave herself the rest of the way up. She let them dangle, not even seeking a toehold.

"What have I done?"

It was Jeffrey's voice, edged with grief and horror, the little-boy, crazy lilt gone. "I killed someone. I killed Kelly. What have I done?"

Kelly could see him in the moonlight, about twenty yards from her, looking like a huddled child, sobbing as if nothing in the world could comfort him. Suddenly he stood, and before Kelly could figure out what was going on, before she could scream or tell him she was still alive, he had jumped over the edge.

Horrified, Kelly watched him tumbling down, looking as she must have looked, like a boneless dummy, an unreal, stuffed thing bouncing like a broken toy.

He missed the bush that had stopped Kelly, continuing to roll down the hillside.

Kelly sobbed as she pushed herself back away from the edge, let go of her hold and slipped down after him.

"You dummy!" she yelled, sliding down the hillside. "Why? I was alive! Why did you have to do that?" But even as she asked the questions, she knew they were unanswerable, or if there were answers, that Jeff had already supplied them.

43

By the time Kelly replaced the fuel line she'd pulled loose, her arms were so dead she fumbled at the simple job, her fingers numb and clumsy. The line seemed as heavy as a battery and as hard to maneuver.

She'd climbed down and back up the slope twice, certain that she was caught in a repetitive nightmare in gym class, struggling to conquer the ropes again and again. The first time she'd climbed down to find a crumpled but conscious Jeffrey. He'd stared at her, his eyes childlike, but he didn't seem intense and feverish like he had earlier. Kelly stayed more than arm's length away from him, just in case, though he looked harmless now, and hurt.

"Hi, Kelly," he'd said. "So we're both dead. I didn't know it hurt so much to be dead."

"It doesn't," Kelly told him. "At least, I'm pretty sure it doesn't. I've never been dead, so I don't know. You're not dead either, Jeff."

"I did something very bad," Jeff said, looking troubled. "I can't think what it was."

"Never mind for now," Kelly said. "Can you move?"

"It hurts."

"Where?"

"Head. Leg. Other leg. Oh . . . everywhere, I guess."

"Are you bleeding?" Kelly asked.

"I don't know."

Kelly had moved closer then, carefully, alert for any sudden attack. She'd checked him as best she could, then had climbed up to the T-bird, lugging water, rags, and her windbreaker back down to Jeff.

"I can't haul you up," Kelly told him. "I'm afraid to move you. And I couldn't, anyway. If you find any place that's bleeding, use the rags to make a bandage. They're clean — more or less. And drink water. I'll get help. And Jeff?"

She reached in the windbreaker pocket, pulling out the small book. She pressed it into his hand, covered him with the windbreaker, and climbed up the hill again, almost crawling, her arms too heavy to move, her body clamoring for rest and attention, something in her chest stabbing with each breath. She was too tired, too numb, too hurt, and too sickened to think or to cry, though she could tell, vaguely, that very soon she would have to do both.

After

"It's Daddy," Susan said, coming quietly into Kelly's room. "Should I tell him about all this? Should I have him call back? And Tad's here. Do you want to see him?"

"I'll talk to Dad first," Kelly said.

Susan handed her the phone. Kelly patted the bed with her free hand, and Susan, surprised, sat.

"Hi, Dad," Kelly said into the phone. "Yes, I've been thinking it over. . . . It sounds like all I'd get to do is change plugs and do the oil, Dad, and I could do that by the time I was eight or so."

Kelly smiled at Susan. "I've been thinking. There is someone else available. A talented mechanic who could work all summer. . . . Yes, of course it's someone you'd enjoy working with. Who? Susan."

She grinned at Susan's look of combined shock and hope. "Of course she can do it!" Kelly said into the phone. "She's my sister, isn't she?" She covered the mouthpiece quickly at Susan's protests and hissed, "Ssh! I'll teach you. They're both simple jobs. It's harder to change a water pump, and you're going to have to do that for me — today! — so you might as well learn tune-ups while you're at it. I can't even put my coveralls on. You'll have to do it. I'll talk you through it."

Kelly listened for a minute, then said, "Of course she'd want to. But here, why don't you ask her yourself?" She held the phone out to her sister.

Susan, her eyes shining with tears, hesitated.

"I know you can do the mechanics," Kelly told her. "The only question is whether you're willing to slug it out with Dad, or if you'd rather just keep on misunderstanding and holding grudges and feeling sorry for yourself."

Susan glared at Kelly, then grinned and grabbed the phone. She told her father hello, listened, then said, "Of course I was interested, Daddy. You just never bothered asking."

Kelly tried not to laugh. It hurt when she laughed. She waved Susan aside and got slowly to her feet. The tape around her ribs was so tight it was hard to get a full breath and she was glad to sink into the wheelchair and wrap a blanket around herself again. She made her way into the living room, maneuvering the chair clumsily.

"You look like a war hero," Tad told her. His voice was light, but his eyes and face were concerned. "Are you supposed to be up?"

"I'm passing out free advice," Kelly said, wheeling herself over to where he sat on the couch. "Do not crack three ribs and then go mountain climbing."

"I don't plan to," Tad said. "Ever. How are you,

Kel?" He reached out and took her hand, his fingers massaging hers automatically. "Hey," he said, pushing up the sleeve of her robe. "You're purple."

"And black and blue," Kelly said. "How's Talia? She was almost hysterical the last I saw her."

"It was a long night," Tad said. "But Talia was doing better by the time her folks showed up to take her home. The psychiatrist talked with her before she left, and I guess she was finally able to convince Talia that Jeff's having some pretty serious problems . . . that it wasn't all just a misunderstanding. Did Susan fill you in on the details?"

"Pretty much, I think," Kelly said, looking sad. "I got in on some of it, between being wheeled to X ray and getting taped and all. Jeff's folks were pretty upset, too. I saw them in one of the halls."

"The psychiatrist said Jeff's in crisis. She also said that's good, because now no one can fool themselves into thinking his problem isn't so bad."

Kelly thought of Jeff's father, angrily denying, then finally believing, sagging like a deflated balloon.

"I still can't believe it," Tad said thoughtfully. "Jeff climbed through the ceiling, all the way from a closet in the gym storage room to the office storage room. To steal a test. Kelly, I know his dad wouldn't have wanted Jeff's success at that price. I can't understand how we can all speak the same language and still get a different message from the one people are sending."

"I saw your father at the ball game," Kelly said. "He was . . . pretty intense. I don't know how to ask this except to be blunt. Is he pressuring you to be the best, too? Are you going to crack up like Jeff did?"

Tad laughed. "Dad doesn't pressure me any more than I pressure him," he said. "You should see me at his company softball games. I'm so obnoxious I can't believe Dad doesn't leave me home. We get excited. But it's different. It's not like what Jeff must have been feeling to steal a test and then do all those things to you."

"He thought I saw him, thought I was playing games and setting traps to catch him. I didn't see him at all, Tad. I didn't know what was going on. He ransacked my locker while I was cleaning up the cheese mess, ransacked my car and my purse. He made a time-fuse thing to start a fire and left it in my trash can when he ransacked my room. He stole my Spanish final so I'd flunk, then took out the screws in the table in the English classroom, and stole my hat. He slashed it up and stuck it under the Ford. I'm not even sure why he did all that . . . to scare me, or warn me, or keep me off guard.

"He was sure I was going to make a public scene, and turn him in. He ruined my Chem book as insurance that I'd never graduate. He figured if I didn't graduate, I'd be stuck at the high school and he'd be safe from me. Then he decided he'd never be safe from me. It's incredible."

Did he try to drown me? she wondered. I didn't think to ask him about that. It doesn't matter now, I guess. Maybe I'd rather not know. "How bad was Jeff hurt?" she asked.

"Physically?" Tad asked. "Broke his left leg, sprained his right ankle. Concussion. Bruised, of course. Not as bad as you. You got the ribs, the shoulder, and a wrenched back and knee along with the bruises. Are you okay? You never did say."

"I'm okay," Kelly said. As okay as I can be after something like that, she thought. "I guess the pressure from his dad to be the best, the guilt over stealing the test, and the pressure of thinking I was out to expose him were just too much," she said. "I wonder if we could have spotted his problems, if we'd known what to look for. I can spot a problem in a car from a mile off, but people still have me baffled."

"I think you're selling yourself short," Tad said. "Jeff had some pretty nice things to say about how you took care of him . . . after he tried to kill you. It scared me to think I almost lost you. It really made me do some thinking. You know I'm going to M.I.T. But I don't want to be that far away from you. What would you think about looking into the mechanics programs in the Boston area?"

"I think I'd have to raise my rates," Kelly told him. "I'd have to pay for an apartment and food and all, plus school. I don't know, Tad. I think we'd better make it through this summer, first, and then see how things are going."

"You're so hardheaded," Tad said. "That's what I love about you."

"Love?" Kelly asked.

"Well, one of the things."

"You're going too fast for me," Kelly said. "I'm

almost over Danny. But I'm a little slow, Tad. I've figured that out about me. I don't fall in love easily. It takes me a long time to make that commitment."

"Me, I've got a long time," Tad said.

Kelly tried not to laugh. It hurt when she laughed. I won't be able to do any work on cars for a long time, she thought. Half the summer, at least. I suppose I could spend the time trying to figure out the mechanical mysteries of people, instead. I could start with Tad.

She shook her head. She was still shaking it when Tad leaned over and very carefully kissed her.

point® THRILLERS

R.L. Stine

- ☐ MC44236-8 The Baby-sitter — $3.50
- ☐ MC44332-1 The Baby-sitter II — $3.50
- ☐ MC45386-6 Beach House — $3.25
- ☐ MC43278-8 Beach Party — $3.50
- ☐ MC43125-0 Blind Date — $3.50
- ☐ MC43279-6 The Boyfriend — $3.50
- ☐ MC44333-X The Girlfriend — $3.50
- ☐ MC45385-8 Hit and Run — $3.25
- ☐ MC46100-1 The Hitchhiker — $3.50
- ☐ MC43280-X The Snowman — $3.50
- ☐ MC43139-0 Twisted — $3.50

Caroline B. Cooney

- ☐ MC44316-X The Cheerleader — $3.25
- ☐ MC41641-3 The Fire — $3.25
- ☐ MC43806-9 The Fog — $3.25
- ☐ MC45681-4 Freeze Tag — $3.25
- ☐ MC45402-1 The Perfume — $3.25
- ☐ MC44884-6 The Return of the Vampire — $2.95
- ☐ MC41640-5 The Snow — $3.25
- ☐ MC45682-2 The Vampire's Promise — $3.50

Diane Hoh

- ☐ MC44330-5 The Accident — $3.25
- ☐ MC45401-3 The Fever — $3.25
- ☐ MC43050-5 Funhouse — $3.25
- ☐ MC44904-4 The Invitation — $3.50
- ☐ MC45640-7 The Train (9/92) — $3.25

Sinclair Smith

- ☐ MC45063-8 The Waitress — $2.95

Christopher Pike

- ☐ MC43014-9 Slumber Party — $3.50
- ☐ MC44256-2 Weekend — $3.50

A. Bates

- ☐ MC45829-9 The Dead Game — $3.25
- ☐ MC43291-5 Final Exam — $3.25
- ☐ MC44582-0 Mother's Helper — $3.50
- ☐ MC44238-4 Party Line — $3.25

D.E. Athkins

- ☐ MC45246-0 Mirror, Mirror — $3.25
- ☐ MC45349-1 The Ripper — $3.25
- ☐ MC44941-9 Sister Dearest — $2.95

Carol Ellis

- ☐ MC44768-8 My Secret Admirer — $3.25
- ☐ MC46044-7 The Stepdaughter — $3.25
- ☐ MC44916-8 The Window — $2.95

Richie Tankersley Cusick

- ☐ MC43115-3 April Fools — $3.25
- ☐ MC43203-6 The Lifeguard — $3.25
- ☐ MC43114-5 Teacher's Pet — $3.25
- ☐ MC44235-X Trick or Treat — $3.25

Lael Littke

- ☐ MC44237-6 Prom Dress — $3.25

Edited by T. Pines

- ☐ MC45256-8 Thirteen — $3.50

Available wherever you buy books, or use this order form.

Scholastic Inc., P.O. Box 7502, 2931 East McCarty Street, Jefferson City, MO 65102

Please send me the books I have checked above. I am enclosing $_____ (please add $2.00 to cover shipping and handling). Send check or money order — no cash or C.O.D.s please.

Name _____

Address_____

City_____ State/Zip_____

Please allow four to six weeks for delivery. Offer good in the U.S. only. Sorry, mail orders are not available to residents of Canada. Prices subject to change.

PT1092